katara

Timur E. Simsek

katara

Thriller

Editorial: Debra D. Stout

Publisher: BoD · Books on Demand GmbH,
Überseering 33, 22297 Hamburg, bod@bod.de
Print: Libri Plureos GmbH, Friedensallee 273,
22763 Hamburg

ISBN: 978-3-8192-4414-8

the music is lost,

the words are gone.

all that remains

is the silence of losses drawn.

PROLOGUE

Welcome back to Milos!

It was pitch black outside. Darkness shrouded the island and gave the air a chilly feel. Sage brushes rustled in the light wind, and owls hooted their nightly songs. Waves rippled against old cobblestones, from which the harbor had been built centuries ago. Light footsteps hurried along the narrow streets as moored boats groaned under the movement of the ocean. Somewhere in the distance, church bells chimed. From a handful of houses, golden light spilled out into the night. For the most part, the islanders were asleep. All but two brothers. One considerably younger than the other. As they went along, they glanced around every corner before making a turn. It seemed as if the entire world was on their heels.

"I don't know about this," the younger brother said wearily.

With his meager ten years, he was young enough to still be scared of the dark.

"It'll be fine. No one will know," the other reassured.

At around eighteen, the older brother still carried the youthful arrogance that made men fearless.

"How can you be so sure?"

"Just trust me, okay?"

The boy stayed silent, and so it was taken as a sign of compliance. The pair made a few more turns here and there until they came upon a house painted in dark red. Above its door, a sign read: Boating Club.

"This is the place?" the eighteen-year-old asked. His accomplice nodded.

"Check the windows!"
Silently, the younger sibling glanced into the house, trying to be as vigilant as possible so as not to be detected.

"See anything?"
The boy shook his head.

"The coast is clear then. Let's move!" Without further ado, the older brother took out a lockpick and inserted it into the keyhole. Fidgeting around for a brief moment, they waited tensely until a clicking sort of noise could be heard. With a victorious smile, the intruder let the door swing back. Jerking his head to the left, he ordered his companion to step inside.

Once past the threshold, the pair went down the corridor before opening a door on the left-hand side. They didn't look for anything else or whether someone was upstairs.

"Is this the door to the basement?" the older brother asked.

"It is."

The two of them had found what they were looking for.

"Here's how we're going to do it. While I go down there to take care of business, you go back to the front door and stand guard."

"And what if someone comes our way, Abi? How do I alarm you?"

"I noticed a vase standing right next to the entrance. If someone is coming towards us, toss it over. The noise will alarm me."

"And then what?"

"You get the hell out of here! I'll do the same, just from out of the basement. We'll link back up at home."

Having understood the plan, and with trembling knees, the brothers shook hands and went their separate ways. One went down to the basement, the other back to the door.

In the end, the little boy couldn't remember for how long he had been standing by the entrance, but when he got there, fog had already crept in and taken hold of the port. Anxiously, his eyes surveilled the plaza, the boats, the houses, and the hallway behind him. Twice, a fluffy grey cat made him jump out of his skin. This entire plan had been a stupid idea from the beginning. But he could never deny his older brother. So, instead, he had been talked into this madness. Silently, he cursed his lack of courage. Having taken his mind off of what he was supposed to do, the kid let himself slide down against the doorframe and stare at the doormat. He was so deep in thought he almost entirely missed the dark-hooded figure having emerged out of the fog. Startled back into reality by the sudden hissing of another cat, the boy looked up and spotted the shadow lurking in the dark. All the way over on the other side of the port, right by a yellow boat, the figure carried a gigantic bag over their shoulders. Intrigued, the child watched closely. What on earth was this person doing? What were they carrying? The shadow continued on with their bag for another couple of meters until they found a big enough niche between two boats. There, and without hesitation, the person suddenly threw the large item into the water. In an effort to see what was happening, the kid got up and moved closer. A fatal mistake. In his mindlessness, he tossed over the exact vase his older brother had mentioned earlier. Alarmed by the noise, the shadow at the other end of the port stopped dead in their tracks. Head jerking up, they immediately detected the boy. Afraid he had given himself away, the youngster ran into the boating club to hide. After what felt like ages, he peeked back out, but by then, the shadow had vanished into thin air...

BROTHERS AT HEART

Inspector Dionisis Lagos was looking at the dead boy's eyes or whatever had been left of them. Selim glanced over his shoulder, a majestic frown on his face. The curly-haired Turk was clearly disapproving of this horrific find. The Inspector and his companion had been out boating the entire day when suddenly they got themselves involved in a tragedy. But every nightmare has its origins...

Their boat whipped faintly in the waves of the turquoise sea. The engine was peacefully humming along. From the two men lying comfortably on the cushioned deck, faint smoke emanated. The smell of 'dirt' blended with the scent of saltwater, grilled meat, and wine. Dirt, *Lat.*

Milosia Purpurea Serenitatis, was a purple plant native to Milos, commonly referred to as dirt. When consumed, it induced a state of profound euphoria, though it occasionally brought on hallucinations and severe depression. Originally discovered in the rugged hills of Milos, it quickly became a much sought-after substance. The plant's strong, pungent aroma was unmistakable – one that lingered in the air like an ancient secret.

Initially having set out in Adamantas, Dionisis Lagos and Selim spent the first couple of hours driving along the coast until they ended up in the shallow, colorful waters right outside the city of Pollonia. There, they stayed for the majority of the day, enjoying nothing more but the company of good books and the connection of brothers at heart.

Lagos exhaled a long, slow breath, watching the

faint wisps of smoke curl into the evening air. The warmth of the day lingered on his skin, and for a while, he simply let himself bask in the moment, the scent of grilled meat and saltwater mixing in the breeze.

"How come you haven't found yourself a wife yet?" he inquired.

Selim pondered over the question for a little while before answering:

"For whatever reason, I don't seem to have what women in this part of the world are looking for in a man."

"Nonsense! You're just not putting yourself out there enough."

"Is that so? And what about you, Abi? Why haven't you settled down?"

"There are only two things every man must truly love; wine and women. But that doesn't mean you need to surround yourself with one or the other constantly. I've found my peace in solitude." Selim laughed heartedly. He had expected exactly that type of answer. With deep wrinkles on his forehead, Dionisis Lagos suddenly leaned forward and sincerely asked:

"Would you consider me to be one of your dearest friends?"

At the same time, he took a considerable puff of his 'drift'. *Drift* was the Melian slang for a hand-rolled cigarette containing dirt, the purple herb that sent the islanders into fits of euphoria and haze.

"You're more than that, Abi. You're my brother!"

Lagos was touched by his friend's statement, for whom he felt the same way. He handed Selim the drift before leaning back into the cushions. He could feel his mind spinning.

"So, how does it feel to be the new big celebrity on the island?" Selim wondered, a teasing glint in his eye. Lagos let out a short chuckle, but the smile faded almost as quickly as it had come. He took another hit of his drift, exhaling through his nose.

He had never cared for attention. Yet, a few weeks after solving the tragic death of Stefanie Sigmund, a Swiss tourist, and after unearthing a long-lost relic called the apple of Hephaestus, Inspector Dionisis Lagos had been awarded the Medal of Outstanding Honorable Services by the Melian police force. Additionally, he had been promoted to Detective Inspector, which was a never-before-seen position. Upon receiving said medal and title in front of thousands of cheering spectators on the island, he was also awarded a mansion on top of the Mellides hill, from where he would overlook the entirety of Adamantas and its outskirts.

"I wouldn't call it that," he muttered. His friend smirked. "Oh? A medal, a mansion, a new title – if that's not celebrity status, I don't know what is."

Lagos hesitated, rolling the drift between his fingers. "I didn't ask for any of this," he admitted, his voice quieter this time. "I just did what I had to do. I solved a case. That's all. I never wanted to be special or different. And yet..." He sighed. "They act like I won some grand prize. Her death is not my glory." Selim studied him for a moment, then nodded, as if understanding the weight his friend carried. With puffy red eyes, legs as heavy as solid rocks, and a mind floating aimlessly in the clouds, their conversation could have lingered in that heaviness, but the sudden jerk under Lagos' seat snapped them both out of it.

"A fish just hooked!"

In his somewhat inebriated state of mind, he started pulling on the rod, but to no avail. It was only a puny fish, barely the size of a toddler's hand. Disappointed, he untangled the animal and threw it back into the ocean. Selim laughed.

"Why get upset about a fish? We have plenty of souvlaki over there," and with that, the young Turk pointed towards the grill in the back. Sizzling and letting off steam, the meat was cooking away.

"You're right!"

Lagos shook his head, then let out a breath of laughter, his earlier frustration momentarily forgotten. As he helped himself to some pita bread, tzatziki, and meat, Selim suddenly got a phone call.

"Who might this be?" he wondered out loud and started fidgeting around himself to find his cell. After a brief instance of struggling, Selim put the phone to his ear and said:

"Merhaba, this is Selim speaking." Lagos couldn't hear who was on the other end, but whoever it was, it certainly wasn't to his friend's liking. The young man's face turned from a happy smile to an expression of concern.

"We'll be there as soon as possible," Selim promised and, with that, hung up the phone. Lagos' mind had sobered up immediately. He knew something was wrong. Alarmed, he waited for his friend to tell him who he had just been talking to.

"It was my cousin, Hakan. He asked for our help!"

"Regarding what?"

"His son has just been found dead by the harbor."

Upon their return to the marina of Adamantas, they noticed a huge commotion by the food market right off the docking stations. A large crowd of onlookers had formed around a fountain depicting Poseidon, the ancient god of the sea. Somewhere, not too far off in the distance, a jazz band was playing their uplifting beats to the dining guests of a pristine hotel.

Arduously, the Detective Inspector made his way through the mob while Selim stayed back to finish docking their boat. He would catch up to Lagos just moments before the latter could breach the safety barrier built by the police around the deceased boy's body. But for now, Dionisis Lagos struggled to get through to the corpse. The pesty gawkers immediately recognized the 'grand Detective Inspector' and naturally wanted to know if he had been assigned to the tragedy that must've occurred. Staying silent, Lagos had to forcefully get over to the statue of Poseidon. Once there, he realized that this was not where the body was. It merely presented itself as the best viewing point for the spectacle. The boy actually lay all the way over by the prominent hotel.

The corpse was heavily guarded by the police force, who tried to keep those spectators at arm's length, who were just a bit too nosey. As they recognized the Detective Inspector, they made way. Right then, Selim caught up to him. Upon entering the secluded bubble, Lagos immediately noticed a crying couple kneeling next to the body. They must've been the parents. On the other side of the cadaver, a female forensics officer was conducting her research. Timidly, Lagos was on the verge of approaching the parents, but before he could, the tearful man recognized Selim and pulled him in a tight hug, sparing the Detective Inspector the need to initiate a conversation. Afterward, Selim hugged the woman. As they did so, they exchanged a few words in their native language. Lagos didn't understand much, as his Turkish skills were ridiculously poor.

"This is my cousin, Hakan Yavuz," Selim explained and lay his hand on the man's back, "and this is his wife, Aylin."

"Then this must be your boy?"

"Yes, this is our son, Kazim."

Aylin broke down in tears again. Naturally, the severity of this situation affected her beyond means of explanation. Lagos bowed his head in condolence before kneeling down to inspect the dead boy more thoroughly. Kazim's eyes had been gouged out, his arms, legs and spine shattered. It appeared as if someone had violently thrown the body against the steps upon which he lay now. He was arranged like a sack of potatoes in the basement. Behind the boy's head was no blood. The entire scene indicated to Lagos that the victim must've died somewhere else. What the Detective Inspector particularly took notice of, however, wasn't the fatality of the crime but rather how it was presented. Even though the boy lay as if he had been passively dismissed, the dead body was dressed fashionably. His hair had been done, and his shoes polished. Lagos turned his head to face the grieving parents:

"Are those your son's clothes?"

"No. We've never seen those before."

"Is there a quiet place we can talk? I need to ask you a few more questions. Normally, we would invite you down to the police station in a few days. However, given the situation, I'd like to get some things out the way right now."

"If you must, you may come by our house." Once done examining the corpse, Lagos got back up and instructed the officer to have the body taken to the forensics office in Adamantas. Selim offered to go with them, as he was one of the most respected pathologists on the island, but Lagos declined. He wanted his curly-haired friend to accompany him to the Yavuz's home.

"I need you as a translator. You'll get your chance to perform your own autopsy of the deceased in due time."

Selim nodded in agreement.

OF PAIN AND SORROW

While the corpse was packed up and sent off to the forensics office, Lagos and Selim walked over to Hakan and Aylin's car. It was a black Lancia, most likely built in the early 2000s. The four of them would drive home to the Yavuzes.

Surrounded by majestic apple trees and great fields of vine, the family manor stood tall on the outskirts of Adamantas. The white facade, with its blue fences, panels, and window shutters, contrasted with the heavy green around it. At first glance, you could tell that the Yavuz family was well off, especially for immigrants. No one spoke as Hakan parked the car on the gravel right in front of the door. Half of the vehicle was still peering out onto the dusty street when Lagos and Selim got out. Immediately, the Detective Inspector noticed a face peering out at him from under a window blind. It vanished as fast as it had appeared.

As the group walked over to the front door and was eventually welcomed in, Selim observed his friend from the corner of his eye. He could tell that Dionisis was absorbing the entirety of this scene, almost like a black hole. Ever since the Hephaestus case, Lagos had been a changed man. Where there had once been an unmotivated, lazy man now stood someone sharp, methodical, and relentless in his pursuit of truth. Hence, the man would take everything in and mold it over for eternity in his brain until he had the solution to this tragedy.

Once inside the house, the guests were asked to be seated on the couch while Aylin went to make tea. Hakan, in the meantime, searched for his oldest son. A few minutes later, he descended back down the stairs with what was a spitting image of himself. Murat Yavuz had the same beady, black eyes as his father, with a striking chin, a light scruff for a beard, and blonde-brown, wavy hair. Overall, with his olive-tainted skin, he was a handsome, genteel young man. As soon as he saw the guests, he came forward and offered up his hand. Dionisis Lagos eyed him well and came to the conclusion that this was not the face he had seen peering out at him a minute ago. The boy was speaking eloquently with an air of cunning about him. Somehow, you could never tell what he was about to say next.

"We would like to talk to you," Lagos explained carefully and with his head tilted, fearing a strong reaction from the teenager. Instead of replying, Murat looked questioningly at his father and then his mother, who had just appeared from out of the kitchen with a tray of black tea.

"Take a seat, Oğlum," Hakan said quietly and motioned for his son to sit down. Just then, it dawned on Murat.

"Where's Kazim?"

While Murat frantically looked around, desperately searching for an answer, his parents each laid a hand on his shoulder. Selim began to kneel in front of the boy, making sure he held eye contact.

"Your brother has been found by the harbor," Selim started, "he is dead."

Lagos, standing behind the couch and leaning with his hands on the cushions, watched as this man, barely more than a boy, collapsed like a house of stacked cards. Lagos' heart tugged. Murat was trying his best to fight back his tears, but it was evident he would break soon.

"Where is he now?" he spoke feebly.

"He's at the forensics office. We will determine his cause of death before he's returned to you".

Silence oozed into the room like a sickness.

"I know this is difficult right now, but do you think I could ask you some questions?" Lagos inquired carefully. Murat merely nodded.

"When's the last time you've seen your brother?"

"Last night. Before I went to bed. Why?"

"What were you up to before going to bed?" Confusion flickered across the young man's face. In Murat's mind, Lagos sensed he was probably wrestling with whether he was seen as a suspect or not. After a brief moment of hesitation, he explained:

"I was out playing football with Kazim. Just right behind the house in one of the fields. We came back here when nightfall set in. We had stuffed bell peppers for dinner before going to bed. Kazim closed the door behind him. That's the last time I saw my..."

Now, at last, the boy's eyes filled with tears. As he was crying, his body twitched.

"So you're certain the two of you came home together?" Lagos asked as he stared insistently at Murat.

"Yes, of course!"

"I can confirm this," Aylin inserted herself into the interrogation, "Murat and Kazim both walked in the front door, all dirty and laughing. I remember because I scolded them for not putting their shoes on the rack."

"So the boy was taken out of his bed," concluded the Detective Inspector. He wondered, did the child know his kidnapper? Did he go willingly?

"Do I have permission to sweep young Kazim's room?" Lagos queried.

A few minutes later, the entire ensemble had made their way upstairs and was now looking at Kazim's room. It was your typical pre-teen environment. Toys clustered on the carpet floor, some posters of a local football club hung on the walls, and a handful of different-sized teddy bears adorned the pillows on the bed. Next to that, a dirty window gave view of the endless-seeming vineyard. Straight across and up against the wall stood a table.

"He used to do his homework here," Aylin explained.

While Lagos stepped further into the room, Selim examined the table. Papers with basic math equations and a couple of notebooks lay scattered across the wooden surface.

"What's this?" Selim asked as he held a tiny wooden boat in the air. It looked old and ragged, with the once-blue color chipping off in certain places. He had found it inside a drawer, next to the boy's underwear.

"I've never seen that before," the parents confessed in unison. Their son agreed as Lagos made a note of it. He was about to continue his examination of the space when Hakan added:

"I'm not sure if this has anything to do with this wooden boat, but Kazim used to work at the boating club down by the docking stations. Here in Adamantas, I mean."

"What was his occupation?"

"He used to be a boat cleaner. It was just a little side job, nothing crazy. But a good first employment for a young man. He would usually go there on Saturdays and help with whatever the club members needed."

Lagos made a mental note of that, too. If foul play was involved, was it connected to someone at the club? Was there perhaps someone who had taken a liking to Kazim, one that went too far? Where did this wooden boat come from? Maybe he had gotten it as a gift at work, Lagos thought as he glanced out of the window for the second time. Nothing out of the ordinary in this room. For reasons he couldn't explain, Lagos felt strongly that something was off, and yet there was nothing to show for it.

Just as he was about to turn around, Dionisis spotted something.

"Do you mind if I take a look at your son's room from outside the house?"

Confused by the vagueness of the question, the Yavuz's granted his wish.

As they all went back down the stairs, Murat looked questioningly at Selim, who only shrugged his shoulders. He was equally as clueless as the others in regard to what was going on. While the group walked around the house to where Kazim's room was, the Detective Inspector abruptly gave a surprised but confident "ha" from him. With large steps, he walked up to what he had discovered and kneeled down.

"Look here, Selim. A shoeprint!" Lagos exclaimed and pointed at the muddy formation. Selim, peering over his colleague's shoulder once more, could now see it too. It was a worker's boot, size forty-two. It was clearly a man's.

THE BOATING CLUB

Lagos and Selim sat outside a café near the harbor. They each drank an espresso. A small dish of baklava and assorted fruits graced their table. While Selim was reading the local newspaper, Dionisis was immersed in deep thought. He was going over what he had witnessed at the Yavuz house. It seemed as if all fingers pointed towards a kidnapping. But, without the forensics office's official report on the cause of death, it was mere speculation. What if the boy had simply run off at night and then drowned in the waters of the port? He might have been attempting to climb on a boat when tragedy struck. Perhaps, people had found him in the waters of the port the next morning before carrying him over to the hotel. The people of Milos were known for their interdependent nature, so this wouldn't have been a surprise to anyone.

"No, no, this doesn't make any sense! How would that explain the post-mortem assault?" the Detective Inspector muttered under his breath. Lagos knew he was wasting his energy by thinking about these things, and yet, his brain just couldn't leave it alone. He needed answers! Glancing at his watch, he suddenly said to his companion:

"It's time."

Without saying a single word, Selim put down his papers and got up. Lagos snatched another baklava and then rose from his chair. Together, they walked across the deserted harbor. A light wind accompanied them as the sails of the colorful boats rustled. Close to the food market, an orange-tabby cat was chasing after a rat. Two elegantly dressed women passed by, talking casually about their respective affairs. As the men approached the dark red house with its letters stating 'boating club' an elderly couple sat feeding pigeons on a bench placed directly in front of the building. While Lagos knocked on the door, Selim smiled at the seniors. No one opened. The Detective Inspector repeated his spiel. Again, no response. Out of curiosity, Lagos tried the door knob. It unlocked seamlessly, and so the men, with raised eyebrows, let themselves in.

Inside, a dim, squeaky light swung back and forth. Immediately after stepping through the doorway, Selim began repeatedly sniffing the air. Something seemed to bother him, but before Lagos could ask, he got interrupted by two shouting men. They were clearly having a heated debate. Walking along the narrow hallway, the Detective Inspector and his companion emerged into a large room. At its center, two middle-aged men were on the verge of a fight. The room was messy, had boating parts scattered everywhere, and the sink on the right-hand side was filled to the brim with dirty plates. This wasn't a high-end boating club like Lagos had expected it to be. Announcing his arrival once more, Dionisis knocked against the wall next to him.

"Yassas, gentlemen," he said loud and clear.

The two men instantly stopped arguing and faced him like two naughty children who had been caught in the act of mischief.

"I hope I'm not interrupting anything," Lagos smiled ironically.

"Not at all! Welcome in! Are you looking to rent a boat?"

The man on the left had spoken and, with that, took a step forward.

"Not per se, no."

"Don't you know who that is, you idiot?" The man on the right had talked now.

"No, I don't! And why should I?" the other returned and faced his rival again.

"That is Inspector Dionisis Lagos! He's the renowned policeman who solved the Hephaestus case."

"Actually, it's *Detective* Inspector now," Lagos inserted himself, his index finger held high. He said so, not necessarily to boast his own ego but to prevent these two fellows from picking up another fight.

"My apologies, Detective Inspector," the man on the right spoke sarcastically, "my name is Marcus Hepburn."

"That's an interesting name for a Greek," Selim noted.

"I'm no Greek, sir. I am American. I moved here from Boston a few years ago."

"And who might you be?" the man on the left inquired, pointing at the curly-haired Turk.

"You can call me Selim."

"My name is Emanuel Lorreant."

"That's also not very Greek," Lagos remarked.

"I'm originally from France."

"That explains the accent."

Confused about whether that was a compliment, Emanuel Lorreant shot Selim a questioning glance.

"What brings you in today, officers?" Marcus asked.

His piercing blue eyes had a hint of insecurity in them. With his messy blonde hair and a patchy, same-colored beard, he looked like a man who had never fully gone past puberty. Emanuel was the complete opposite. He dressed elegantly in a suit and tie, his hair was combed back, and he was clearly shaving every morning, according to the rash on his neck at least. Both roughly around the same height and with the same set of eye colors, they could've easily been mistaken as estranged twins.

"Have you ever heard the name 'Kazim Yavuz'?"

"Of course! He's the lovely young man who helps out at the club on weekends," Emanuel stated, and a happy smile showed on his face. The speed of this reply was certainly something Lagos would remember.

"Why are you asking about him?"

"He's been found dead by the port."

Purposely pausing, Dionisis observed the men's reactions. They couldn't have been more different from each other. While Marcus Hepburn's face stayed completely mellow to the point of apathy, Emanuel Lorreant was clearly devastated. As the latter wrung with his hands, he remained on the brink of shedding a tear. Lagos inquired:

"When's the last time you've seen Kazim?" While Lorreant tried to get a hold of himself, Hepburn clarified that he had talked to the boy the day before his passing. He had offered him an apprenticeship as a sailor. He continued on explaining that Kazim had been working at the boating club for a while and that everyone was fond of the young, enthusiastic child.

"I can attest to that. Kazim was such a lovely, bright young lad who was truly devoted to his work here," Emanuel Lorreant added, with a fondness in his voice attempting to push back the sorrow he felt.

"He was a good kid, indeed. Surprisingly, given his family. But, because he was so popular with the staff and our customers, the board decided to give him the position as an apprentice." Marcus Hepburn's remark seemed to throw off Selim, who reacted with disdain.

"How did he react to that?"

"He looked overjoyed! Apparently, he had been hoping for a position with the boating club for when he would turn old enough to work officially."

"What's with the animosity against Turks, Mr. Hepburn?" Selim inserted himself. Lagos knew that question was bound to be dropped, given his friend's facial expression earlier.

"There's no animosity, sir. I'm just a firm believer that his family should've stayed back in Turkey."

"What are your positions here at the club, if I may ask?" Lagos interrupted in an effort to defuse the situation. He could tell that Selim was on the verge of an antagonistic response.

"I'm the president and a member of the board," Marcus explained.

"And I'm a member here. Perhaps you have noticed my yacht when you got here? The white one? With a jacuzzi on the stern?" Emanuel spoke. Selim shook his head.

"Kazim used to spend a lot of time cleaning my boat. It was his favorite," Emanuel explained with child-like admiration. While Mr. Lorreant went into an anecdote about how Kazim had once asked if he could join for a Sunday afternoon ride, Selim and Lagos eyed each other suggestively.

"What have you gentlemen been arguing about when we came in earlier?"

"That's none of your concern," Mr. Hepburn snapped.

"It may very well be."

"I doubt it."

Lagos accepted that he wouldn't get any more information out of them. Mr. Hepburn's harsh reaction caused Mr. Lorreant to stop his splendid story about young Kazim. Instead, he now eyed the Detective Inspector sheepishly. Dionisis Lagos was about to announce their goodbyes when a woman entered the boating club. She had light-brown hair that was partly covered by a large sun hat. With her brown sunglasses, she wore a matching airy dress. "Mon Amour, it is getting way too hot to sunbathe out there on the yacht. I just wanted to let you know I'm heading home now," she announced as she marched down the hallway. She was in the middle of another sentence when she stopped dead in her tracks. Having taken her shades off, she beheld the Detective Inspector and his companion. "Amélie, Mon Coeur, may I introduce you to Detective Inspector Lagos and the pathologist Selim," said Emanuel as he went over to place a kiss on her cheek. She shook each of their hands respectfully. Amélie Lorreant inquired about their visit, to which Lagos explained the situation. She exclaimed her concerns and offered up her help, but made it clear that she knew of nothing.

On the way out, Selim wondered if Kazim's death might have been a hate crime. To Lagos, it was unsurprising that his friend had come to that conclusion based on Marcus Hepburn's unfriendly opinion of Turks.

"We can't say for certain yet. We must first determine the boy's cause of death."

While Lagos spoke, Selim noticed the peculiar smell again. But this time, too, he simply couldn't pin point it. He wanted to address the issue when suddenly he got another phone call. Apparently, the forensics office had come up with a report on Kazim's death.

Not long after, the pair stood in the center of a deeply sterilized room, towering over the naked, pale body of a roughly ten-year-old boy. A shy-looking woman handed Selim a collection of documents. She smiled at him. As she did so, Lagos smirked.

"Would you like to cross-check the results, sir?"

Her voice was feeble but sweet.

"Gladly," Selim replied and returned her smile.

He quickly put on a pair of plastic gloves and went

to work. As he did so, he compared the body to the report. Repeatedly and at odd intervals, Selim nodded and gave off a faint "yes." After a thorough examination, he turned to face both Lagos and the woman.

"What is written in this report is absolutely correct. The boy died of suffocation. However, a substantial level of water was found in his lungs. It only leaves the possibility that the body was thrown into the waters of the port to dispose of it. This, of course, is only an assumption, as the discovery of the corpse was made on the steps to the hotel. Either way, from the corpse, it can also be determined that Kazim had been sexually assaulted after he met his tragic end. He must've died within the last forty-eight hours. The boy's cause of death is homicide." With that, Selim closed his report.

Lagos fell into a deep silence. It was evident that he was churning something over in his mind.

"Why would they throw him into the water in the first place? Why not leave him by the hotel if that is the whole point? This doesn't add up!"

"I can answer that question. Some passersby apparently observed a figure fishing in the port. They thought the person was trying to save someone from drowning," the woman explained. As it turned out, she had been the forensics officer who had worked the crime scene at the hotel. After the body was sent off, she decided to talk to some of the civilians.

"You're saying someone purposely placed the boy on those steps? Maybe the killer came back to change the way police would find him." After thinking such horrific things out loud, the Detective Inspector fell back into silence.

"Was it a man or woman who killed this boy?" he finally asked.

"We cannot say. Due to the salt water, the assault marks have eroded too far."

Lagos' eyes stayed sternly fixed on the boy's corpse. He then wanted to know:

"Do you remember how we found the boy?"

"Yes. He was well groomed and wore fancy clothes."

"Indeed. The way he was presented in death had an almost motherly touch, don't you think? As if the murderer had made the child pretty for Charon."

THE PASSING OF TIME

Hours turned into days, days turned into a felt eternity. A week had passed since Lagos and Selim had visited the boating club. The island had been experiencing somewhat cooler temperatures. For the Greeks, it was freezing; for anyone else, it was comfortable late summer weather. Clouds rolled in and hung gloomy during the day. Nights, however, could still be spent out on the balcony, sipping white wine and eating dates. Even now, one could hear the laughter of people socializing on the various plazas. Further out, the grapes in the vineyards were about ready to be harvested. Fewer tourists and boating tours meant that a more laid-back, borderline lazy vibe had gripped the mood of the islanders. Even the many animals strolling the streets seemed more drowsy than usual.

Both Lagos and Selim continued their investigation but to no avail. Wherever they went, whoever they talked to, everyone seemed to have been fond of Kazim Yavuz. He had no issues, no rivals among his peers, nothing. He had been bound to grow up in a healthy social environment. So, who on earth wanted to harm this young man?

High up in his mansion, overlooking Adamantas and its immense outskirts, Detective Inspector Dionisis Lagos was getting restless. Never before in his entire career had it happened that his investigation met a dead end. Apart from the boating club, there was no lead to follow, no inkling of what might have happened. It was as if Kazim had been murdered by a ghost. Lagos had experienced this before - hitting a plateau with his cases or that he was missing a piece of the puzzle, and usually, all he had to do was wait. Just as a lion hides in a bush for the impala to draw close enough, he simply had to lay low for his strike. For some reason, his gut told him that the longer he waited, the more this case would slip into unresolved obscurity. Something Lagos was determined to prevent. To give up hope was a man's last resort. Naturally, he turned to the only thing a fellow of his kind could do. He ordered multiple carafes of Greek wine, heaps of food and invited his most recent romantic pursuit over for a visit. Given his constant sway between longing for company and seeking solitude, he had been neglecting her lately. To his surprise, she appreciated his call and left her place immediately.

As such, Lagos was snuggling with a local brunette when his dearest friend Selim burst into the front door. As the Turk entered, food was cooked in the marble kitchen, the TV was on, and somewhere in the back, one could hear the water running for a steamy bath.

"Abi, it's urgent!" the young Turk shouted. Startled, the woman in Lagos' lap jumped. With a self-perceived feeling of having been caught in the act, she got up and went to the bathroom. Lagos, in the meantime, casually stretched himself out on his couch. Neither Selim nor he addressed what had just happened.

"What is it, Selim?"

"Another boy has been found dead by the harbor."

"To hell with all of this!" Lagos exclaimed and spat on the ground. Selim, who stood next to him, agreed. They had immediately made for the port. Barely less than twenty minutes ago, the Detective

Inspector was enjoying life's riches to the fullest, and now he stood here, towering over another dead boy. This one was barely older than Kazim Yavuz. Once more, the deceased had been elegantly dressed with the tenderness of a mother's hand, only to be tragically subjected to the bestial disposal of a heartless father. Unlike the first victim, who was found in front of the pristine hotel, this one lay on the steps to the jazz club. At first glance, it could be observed that the boy's clothes were soaked. Most likely, some Samaritans had fished the poor soul out of the water. As Lagos approached the body for proper inspection, the sun vanished behind the horizon, dipping the sky in a palette of dark orange and pink. A small crowd of onlookers had again gathered around the policemen. Finding dead boys on the steps of prominent venues wasn't an everyday occurrence to most people on Milos. As such, morbid curiosity was unsurprising. Selim started glancing around, moving from left to right in even intervals.

"There's a drug store, a hotel, a jazz club, and a supermarket nearby," he explained.

"So you've had the same thought as I?"

"The bodies have been purposely placed on the steps of certain venues? In turn, connecting them to this conundrum?"

"Exactly."

"Then yes, Abi, I have."

Was it truly a message from the killer that one boy was found by the hotel and another by the jazz club? If there would turn up another body tomorrow, would it land on the same steps or perhaps on the steps of the drugstore? Or was it all but a coincidence? Either way, it was a lead, and that was something Lagos was starving for.

"Lend me your forensic eye, Selim. Do you see any anomalies?"

While Selim knelt down to study the boy properly, Lagos, in turn, got back up. He was about to write a peculiarity down in his booklet when an elderly man approached him with the words:

"You're that detective everyone's talking about, eh?"

"Unfortunately, yes. I'm Detective Inspector Dionisis Lagos."

"My name is Nikos Zeniades," he spoke. Nikos Zeniades was most likely as ancient as the Greek gods. He was bald, except for three long, rumpled grey hairs on the top of his head. He was missing a front tooth and had bad breath in general. His crossed eyes were faintly grey, looking much like a lunatic going blind. Leaning on his light brown cane, he added:

"I'm a fisherman. I've been working these waters for the past forty years."

"That's great. What can I do for you, Nikos?"

"You can pay attention to what I'm about to tell you. I'm the one who found the boy!" Starstruck, the Detective Inspector stared at old Nikos.

"What do you mean by that?"

"You see, I was out fishing the entire day. Once the sun began settling, I returned. During the process of entering the harbor with my daily catch, the engine suddenly got stuck on something. My efforts to untangle whatever it had been that got caught in the turbines ended in terror. To my shock, I held a boy in my arms."

"What did the corpse look like when you first found it?"

Lagos looked at Nikos inquisitively. The old man hesitated. He appeared to be kick-starting his grey cells into conjuring up vivid imagery.

"He was all blue and bloated. His eyes were messed up. Other than that, he had deep, shredded cuts in his body, but I assume those to be from my boat's turbine."

Lagos nodded. While the Detective Inspector remained silent, working over the new information, Selim joined them and asked:

"Are you the one who placed the boy on the steps to the jazz club?"

The curly-haired Turk had overheard their conversation.

"I was not. I merely dropped him off at the docking station. I left him unattended to finish tying up my ship. When I turned back around, the corpse was gone! You see, at my age, I can't be bothered with these smartphones anymore, so I had no means of contacting anyone out on the sea. I was planning on telling people here that they should go get help, but alas! You see what happened when I turned my back."

In utter bewilderment, Dionisis started frantically looking about. That could only mean one thing! The murderer was here! He had observed poor Nikos drop off the boy, and when the old man had turned his back, the killer swept in to relocate the corpse to the club.

"How long did it take you to finish docking the boat, Nikos?"

"Not sure. Maybe two minutes."

"Impossible!" Selim muttered.

His mind had jumped to the same conclusion as that of his friend.

"Did I say something wrong?" Nikos asked, uncertain of what had just happened.

"Not at all. Is there anything else you'd like to tell us?"

"No, sir," and with that, the fisherman said his goodbyes and went back to his boat. In a hurry, Selim bent down to inspect the cuts, those mentioned by Nikos, while Lagos remained standing. His back turned to the corpse, he scanned the entire harbor. With some luck, he might spot the suspect. But he considered his chances slim; after all, the harbor, as well as the plaza and the adjacent fish market, were now crowded with people wanting to enjoy the mild, late summer evening.

"Oh no, how tragic! I knew this boy," a man exclaimed, standing right next to Lagos. The figure had appeared from out of the crowd of onlookers. His head held low, and with a face that displayed thoughtfulness, he then faced Lagos.

"Who might you be?"

"Sorry, I haven't introduced myself properly. My name is Adonis Markas."

Lagos shook his hand.

"Who's the boy?"

"This is Noah Hepburn."

"Marcus Hepburn's son?"

"So you two know each other?" Adonis inquired, unable to hide his astonishment. Adonis Markas was a man with feminine facial features and a slim build. He wore a pair of light-brown linen pants and a black button-up shirt. His sleeves folded back, he had his hands on his hips.

With his long, curly hair and clean-shaven face, he was a fine-looking man. His grey eyes turned most people to stone as if cursed by Medusa.

"We've met," Lagos returned, "and you're certain this is his son?"

"Absolutely! He's a good friend of my son, Paris".

"When's the last time Paris and Noah talked?"

Adonis expressed his uncertainty. Paris would often meet his friends at the playground, so he was unsure of when his son had last seen the deceased.

"Could I talk to your son about this?"

"Of course! I own the coffee shop called 'Demeter' out by Lagada Beach. You may come by anytime you want."

Lagos promised that he would. Content with that, Adonis left to finish running some errands while the Detective Inspector shifted his focus to the now-identified corpse.

He watched as forensics wrapped Noah Hepburn's body in a zip bag.

LACHRYMOSE

"Marcus needs to be informed about his son's death," Selim urged, looking over at his friend Dionisis, who was leaning against the garden railing, facing the city. Together, they stood in the yard of the Detective Inspector's mansion. Behind them, two workers were tending to the lawn. One was occupied with the pool, the other trimming some delicate flowers. Realizing that Lagos was not going to answer, Selim turned around to face the workers.

"The state even cleans your place! What outrageous luxury."

"Have it all! I want none of it!"

Selim scrutinized his counterpart. Lagos knew what his friend wanted to know, so he said:

"I've been cursed with this mansion. They reward me with pompous goods and titles to honor my outstanding deeds. But I haven't done anything grand. I merely did my job, and a poor one at that, if you ask me. Now, I'm facing my punishment."

"Horrible indeed, not even having to tidy up anymore. But why would you say that? Others would kill for your riches!"

Lagos remained silent for a while. As his eyes lingered on the lights of the city, he replied:

"Everything here serves as a persistent symbol of my shortcomings. Had I performed my duties meticulously, no lives would have been lost on this island. This house consistently highlights my inability to ensure people's safety. I was unable to protect Stefanie Sigmund from her tragic fate, and now I'm finding myself unable to shield these young boys from life's cruelty.

Let me ask you this, Brother; what good does a mansion do up in the skies, so far removed from reality that my own helping hand can't reach those in need anymore?"

"Depends on how you look at it, Abi. Now that you own more resources, instead of spending it all on yourself to erase your misery, you could instead put it into places that need your help."

As the two men continued discussing, dark, heavy clouds rolled in from the east. Rain would soon set in. The smell of damp grass and pavement hung in the air. Understanding that there was much to do, the Detective Inspector and the pathologist decided to first pay a visit to Mr. Hepburn. If the police hadn't done it yet, they would be the first ones to break the horrible news to him.

Mr. Hepburn lived in a decent-sized, modern house on the eastern banks of Adamantas. His home was directly built on the beach, his terrace facing the light-blue waters of the Aegean Sea. Lagos and Selim both walked up to the front door and rang the bell. They were greeted by a woman in her mid-forties. With her ashen-blonde hair, she was lovely to look at. Based on the heavy, dark rings around her green eyes, one could tell that she hadn't slept at all in the past few days. Now facing the two men, she instinctively knew why they had come.

"My name is Detective Inspector Lagos. This is my colleague Selim from the forensics office. May we come in for a moment?"

She merely nodded and made way for them to step inside. As the Detective Inspector did so, he asked:

"Who do I have the pleasure with?"

"My name is Anna Hepburn," she said with a strain of tiredness in her voice, "please go up the stairs and to the right. My husband is out on the balcony. I reckon you want to talk to us both?"

"Indeed."

Selim, who made way for Anna to lead the way, could see how she shuddered upon Lagos' agreeing with her inquiry.

The terrace was spacious, tidy, and decked with lots of elegant furniture. Marcus Hepburn was lying on the divan, his head facing the ocean. Helping himself to some grapes, he was clearly in deep, worried thought.

"Good afternoon, Marcus," Lagos opened the conversation.

The sight of the two policemen standing there pushed the once stone-cold face to the verge of tears.

"It's true then," he spoke without taking his eyes off them.

"Anna, please take a seat," Selim requested and motioned her to sit next to her husband. Once she was situated, Lagos said:

"We've found Noah on the steps to the jazz club."

While Anna broke down into tears, Marcus remained cold. No parent should ever have to experience the heart-wrenching news of their own child's death. Selim's empathetic eyes rested on Anna as her body shivered and trembled. Lagos silently observed the husband. He looked spaced out, miles away in thought. Dionisis would have to ask them some questions, but he wanted to allow them to let everything sink in. Leaving the parents to their grief, the Detective Inspector took a seat across from the divan on a comfortable chair. Afterward, he couldn't remember for how long he had been sitting there, but eventually Marcus asked:

"Where is our boy now?"

"He's at the forensics office. We're trying to determine his cause of death as we speak," Selim explained dryly. His voice let on that he hadn't forgotten his last encounter with the bigoted Mr. Hepburn. Accordingly, he was on edge.

"Is there anything you need to know from us?"

It was Anna who had asked.

Lagos wanted to know when exactly Noah had gone missing. With his hands folded, he slid forward in his chair and put his elbows on his knees. Anna replied:

"Today, exactly one week ago."

"Do we have two different murderers on our hands?" Lagos wondered as he drove over to the prominent hotel. Selim was submerged in a book. His dusty 1970s silver Mercedes was hot and sticky. The air conditioning had recently given up life, and rolling down the windows wasn't of much help either. They had left the Hepburn house after some more questioning. Perhaps Lagos had pushed the two of them too much. Anna, at some point, was so upset that she couldn't formulate any more words through the rain of tears. Something that angered Marcus so much that he shooed them out. During the conversation with Noah's parents, Lagos had made a worrying observation. A thought he simply couldn't shake loose.

"What do you mean?" Selim wondered, still reading.

"I'm simply trying to figure out if the two cases are connected."

"Of course they are!"

"How can you be so sure?"

"Abi, what are the odds of having two dead boys, roughly around the same age, turn up dead in an almost identical fashion?"

"I'm not sure. Either way, I just find it peculiar that Noah was held for seven days straight before being murdered and found. Meanwhile, Kazim vanishes for less than twenty-four hours before turning up dead by the harbor. This speaks for two entirely different MOs. And if it is the same person, then why the discrepancy? In that case, Kazim's death feels rushed compared to Noah's, no?"

Selim did not have an answer.

After arriving at the port once more, the two decided to split up. While Selim took care of the drug store and the supermarket, the Detective Inspector would talk to the hotel employees and the jazz club owners to see if there was any connection between the establishments and the location where the boys had met their ghastly ends.

The hotel lobby unfolded before Dionisis Lagos like an opulent symphony of architectural finesse and artistic allure. The majestic entranceway was flanked by towering columns of polished marble. The foyer boasted a cathedral-like ceiling that soared to dizzying heights, adorned with delicate chandeliers that cast a soft, golden hue upon the scene below. Natural light followed the Detective Inspector as he made his way over to the receptionist. A subtle scent of citrus and florals danced lightly in the air. The murmur of hushed conversations blended with the gentle strains of ambient music. Lagos grimly walked over to the worker, a young, enthusiastic-looking lady.

"Yassas, my name is Detective Inspector Lagos. I'm looking to find some information on the recently found child on your doorstep."

"Certainly! I'll try to assist you as best as I can."

"Great! Could you tell me whether a family by the name of Yavuz has stayed here recently?" The receptionist punched multiple different parameters into her computer. After a brief moment, she said:

"I'm sorry, sir. I must disappoint you. No family by the name of Yavuz has ever stayed here."

"What about the name Hepburn? Also, a family."
Again, she started sifting through her system. This
time around, her eyes lit up with excitement.

"Yes, there is a family of four by the name
of Hepburn who stayed here three months ago."

"Not anytime sooner? Perhaps, like a week
ago?"

"No, sir."

Lagos fell silent, his gaze lingering on the polished
surface of the desk, where shadows stretched like
cracks in his resolve. The receptionist watched
quietly, sensing the weight of unspoken thoughts.

"Could you tell me the names of all family
members?"

"Certainly. It's Frank, Susan, Molly, and
Peter. They came in from Canada."

"I had a hunch. That's not the family I'm
looking for."

The receptionist searched through her files once more.

"I'm sorry, sir. That is the only family called Hepburn who has stayed with us for the past year." Accepting his defeat, Lagos thanked her for her efforts and left the hotel. It was a dead end. Back out on the street, the Detective Inspector bumped into Selim.

"How was your search?" the young pathologist asked.

"Fruitless. Just like yours, I assume?"

"Yup."

There was only one more establishment they had to pay a visit to. Together, they walked into the jazz club. A cloud of cigar smoke and old leather chairs welcomed them in. Unlike the hotel, this place was dingy and dark. Only a few lights shone brightly on the stage. No one was performing. A middle-aged man with traces of consumption and a hefty grey mustache approached them with open arms. Slightly bowing, he said:

"Welcome in, gentlemen! Care for a drink?"

"We'd care much more for some information."

After briefly introducing themselves, Lagos got straight to the point and asked if either a family by the name of Yavuz or Hepburn had frequented his place. The owner negated.

"We have a small amount of clients here. It's primarily regulars or borderline seniors at best."

"Are there any odd characters?" Lagos inquired.

"Not that I can think of. The only queer people coming to mind right now are the Lorreants."

"In what way are they odd?"

"Well, Madam Lorreant works as a professor of child psychology at the University of Adamantas, and Mr. Lorreant is the coach of the local football team. I can hear them discuss children a lot whenever they come here." Lagos found this to be profoundly peculiar. It appeared that Mr. Lorreant was somehow connected to both deceased boys. In Kazim's case, Emanuel Lorreant belonged to the same club where the young boy had worked. As for Noah, Lorreant frequented the establishment where the boy's body was later found.

"I would love to know if Noah played football," Lagos thought out loud.

Their final task on the agenda was to stop by the Yavuzes. Upon getting out of the dusty Mercedes, Lagos and Selim could hear shouting coming from inside the house. Clearly, someone was having an argument. As the Detective Inspector and his companion drew closer to the door, it became clear that Hakan and his son Murat were engaged in a heated discussion.

"Yazıklar olsun sana!", Hakan shouted. Questioningly, Lagos peered over at his friend. Selim translated: "He called him a disgrace." Dionisis decided to ring the doorbell, but the voices inside were too loud for anyone to hear. Selim tried the doorhandle. It opened, and so the two men entered the house.

Hakan and Murat stood in the living room, both poised like wolves, ready to lunge at each other. Shouting in Turkish, their heads were deep red and ready to explode.

"Gentlemen! What is going on in here?" Lagos intervened.

Caught completely off guard by the unexpected arrival of an uninvited guest, they promptly seized their verbal fight.

"How did you get in here?" Hakan hissed.

"The front door?"

Startled, Hakan glared at Lagos while Selim asked once more about what was going on. Neither of them seemed willing to provide an answer.

"Why are you so upset, Hakan?" Selim pressed again, this time with more tightness in his voice.

"I found this in my son's drawers, that's why!"

Hakan threw a wad of cash and a small bag of dirt into Lagos' arms. All eyes turned on the young man. At first, Murat appeared to be estimating whether he should be honest or deny the allegations, but then he confessed to consuming dirt.

"I smoke occasionally, okay? I bought it from a friend. I'm sorry."

Humiliated by being forced to make this confession, he ran up to his room. It was almost like a child caught in the act, whose pride had been wounded and who now stumbled off in a fit of rage. Lagos wondered why an adolescent would feel so guilty about smoking a simple drift? Why throw a temper tantrum like that?

"What kind of job does your son have? That's quite a lot of money," Selim asked in astonishment.

"He doesn't have a job, and he refused to say where the cash came from," Hakan explained and shook his head in disbelief. But, the Detective Inspector knew he had more pressing concerns at hand than the money sources of a teenager. So, instead, he turned to face the father:

"Would you consider yourself to be friends with a certain Marcus Hepburn?"

"What? No, not really. Why?"

"He talked about you. But not in the most favorable way."

Unbeknownst to anyone but Lagos, Selim shot his friend an intrigued glance. Where was he going with this?

"Others don't like me? So what! Most people don't even like themselves."

Hakan seemed genuinely annoyed. Lagos continued:

"What can you tell me about Mr. Hepburn?"

"Not much. He's the president of the boating club. My son used to work for him."

"Indeed. But what else?"

"He's also on the city council and the head of infrastructure for Adamantas. But what's that got to do with anything?"

"It's relevant for a rivalry that I cannot comprehend just yet. For some reason, Mr. Hepburn and you aren't fond of each other. But why? Your son was doing a great job at the club, so what could possibly be the reason? Care to tell me? I'm sure you know the answer, Mr. Yavuz." Hakan was chewing his lower lip. Just like Murat earlier, he seemed to be weighing his options. Grudgingly, he explained that Marcus Hepburn had been against Hakan and Aylin building their house. Hepburn would hand in complaints and refuse to give his consent to the project. At one point, the city council as a whole had to vote over the development plans. Luckily, the majority spoke out in favor of the Yavuz's building their home.

During construction, Mr. Hepburn would repeatedly show up unannounced and point out norm violations at any opportunity, delaying the process every time.

"Do you have any idea of why he would behave this way?" Selim inquired. Hakan merely shook his head.

"He believes all Turks are heathens. That's all there is to it."

After Aylin had served them all dinner, something Murat purposely missed out on, the Detective Inspector and his colleague left the house. Lagos was drowsy from all the excellent food. He was still fantasizing about the mantı (Turkish tortellini), the cacık (a yogurt-based soup with cucumbers), the lahmacun (Turkish pizza), and the grilled vegetables. Selim, on the other hand, was staring out into the bare land. A few meager sheep were grazing on one of the planes. The dry, light-brown earth contrasted with the deep blue sky of the early night. The stars patiently waited to shine in the dark.

"Was Marcus Hepburn prying around the house the night Kazim vanished?" Selim pondered out loud.

"I've had the same thought before, too, my friend. It only bears the question; why?"

A FAMILY'S OMINOUS PAST

"Persistent Manhunt Continues for Elusive Pedophile, Island Community on Edge" – read the title of the morning newspaper. Somehow, the information leaked that the police were still looking for the killer of both Kazim and Noah. Unsurprisingly, the entire affair had blown up to become a national sensation, and thus, plenty of journalists and reporters started flooding Milos, hoping to catch any islander willing to talk to them. As it would turn out, Emanuel Lorreant seemed to be quite the goldmine in that regard. He didn't shy away from any interview, elucidating to the entirety of Greece the urgency of capturing this 'bogeyman.'

He apparently enjoyed the attention and his five seconds of fame.

Lagos and Selim couldn't be bothered less. They were too busy catching a murderer. To increase their efficiency, Selim had gone off to the forensics office to assist them in their analysis of Noah's corpse. Meanwhile, Lagos drove over to the city archives. He was hoping to fill in the missing gaps of information so that he could put the different puzzle pieces together.

The Detective Inspector parked his dusty Mercedes right in front of the city archives. The structure was ancient. Quite literally. Having been built in 218 BC, it was the oldest building on the entire island. With white marble pillars and a pointed roof, the building stood tall against the passing of time. Lagos would've loved nothing more as a child than to come here and spend his days reading about epochs long gone.

After talking to the librarian, Lagos made his way down into the basement. The shelves there were stacked with folders and files, primarily concerning city affairs. Somewhere in the back, buried underneath a heap of dust, the Detective Inspector found what he was looking for. A document that stated:

Date: June 14, 2005

Subject: Authorization for Land Development Project

Dear Mr. Marcus Hepburn,

Dear Mr. Hakan Yavuz,

This document serves as an official authorization for the commencement of the land development project situated at Pantelis Saris Street 12 within the city limits of Adamantas.

Mr. Hakan Yavuz has diligently provided all necessary documentation and complied with the prerequisites essential for the initiation of the aforementioned land development project. His commitment, adherence to regulations, and compliance with the city's requirements have been duly acknowledged and confirmed.

It has come to the attention of the City Council of Adamantas that Councilman Marcus Hepburn, the Head of Infrastructure, initially expressed concerns regarding said affair. However, following a comprehensive and deliberative session held by all representatives, a majority vote has been reached. The council mandates Mr. Hepburn to approve the inauguration of this project.

In adherence to the decision made by the City Council, it is imperative that Mr. Hepburn, in his capacity, facilitates and collaborates in ensuring the smooth initiation and execution of the project in question. All relevant departments under his jurisdiction are expected to extend their cooperation and assistance.

Furthermore, any hindrance or delay caused by non-compliance or reluctance to adhere to this directive will be considered a violation of official responsibilities and may result in legal action.

Your understanding, cooperation, and prompt execution are highly appreciated.

Sincerely,

The City Council of Adamantas

This was the root of their feud – Lagos thought. Marcus Hepburn had most likely never gotten over this rectification. In his mind, though, such an embarrassment couldn't possibly be a good enough reason to murder your rival's child. Or could it?

To get clarity, Dionisis Lagos left the city archives and drove over to see Marcus and Anna Hepburn at their house.

Sadness hung in the air as Lagos entered the house. Husband and wife sat on the couch. The TV was running, but neither one of them paid any attention to it. Silently, the parents sat there and mourned. Worn out and pale, both of them looked like they hadn't slept or eaten in days. First, Lagos tenderly inquired about their mental health and how they coped with it all, before asking:

"Explain to me one thing, Marcus. Why were you against the Yavuz's building their house?"

"Never said I was."

"The letter of authorization I found at the city archives paints a different picture."

"Okay, yes. Perhaps I wasn't a fan of the project. So what?"

"It's just that when I asked Mr. Yavuz who could potentially have a motive to kill his son, his mind immediately jumped to you. Why?" This statement of his wasn't entirely fact-based, of course, but Lagos wanted to see how the Hepburns would react to the idea of it.

"That old fool!" Marcus roared. However, he made no attempt to deny the Detective Inspector's allegation. Lagos purposely waited before expounding his theory:

"I believe you've never moved on from the fact that you were overruled by the city council. Maybe you even convinced yourself by now that

Hakan and Aylin paid corruption money to the board so that they would walk away victorious. And maybe, just maybe, you've kidnapped and murdered young Kazim in an act of retaliation."

"How dare you!"

Marcus had, by now, jumped to his feet. Angrily, he had put his left fist on his hip while he pointed with his right index finger at Lagos. His narrow eyes glared viciously.

"I said 'maybe'. I never claimed to have any evidence. But, your reaction sure is compelling."

Almost as if he had been caught red-handed, Marcus sat back down. Now, calm as a serene lake on a windless day, he admitted:

"Alright, it's true. I did want to own that piece of land back then."

"Why?"

"As an investor myself, I believed to have stumbled upon a goldmine. Inspector, allow me to explain— my roots run deep in this community. I've dedicated years of hard work, significant financial investments, and personal commitment to Milos' growth. I've poured many of my resources into numerous projects that have substantially contributed to the development of this island. If not for my philanthropy, Adamantas might still be underdeveloped. So, genuinely, I believe in having a right to the best parcels of land around here."

"But the Yavuz house is on the outskirts. There's nothing much to it."

"That's where you're wrong. It would've been the perfect spot to build a hotel. Walking distance from the beach and the markets, but far enough to have some peace and quiet, too. Think about the amount of tourists this site would've attracted each season. The revenue generated could've been used to further invest into infrastructure, education, or the reduction of the mafia's influence around these parts."

"So that's why you said the Yavuz's should have better stayed back in Turkey when we came to see you at the boating club."

"Exactly! I never despised Hakan or his family, and I would never harm his boy. My interests solely lie in the well-being of the people on this island, so naturally, I mourn over the potential that was lost when they came here and built their house. But this entire feud is in the past. If Hakan still believes there's any animosity between us, then he's simply a resentful moron." Lagos eyed Mr. Hepburn intensely. The way Marcus grabbed his wife's hand following his words did seem like a heavy burden got lifted off his chest.

Soon after, Lagos said his farewells and left. Just as the front door closed behind him, a call from Selim came in.

"Abi, you need to come to the forensics office right now! It's urgent!"

BENEATH SHALLOW SURFACES

Not long after, Lagos entered the forensics office of Adamantas. It hadn't changed much since his last visit. White and sterile, it made Lagos feel cold and disconnected. Perhaps for the employees, it helped to disassociate with the corpses. See them less as people and more as human-sized clay objects to cut into.

Selim waited by the door. He seemed to be in a frenzy. After hurriedly shaking hands, they made their way through the dimly lit halls and into the back, where they stored the latest arrivals. A woman, roughly forty years old, was cleaning up one of the tables. When she saw the two men come in, she immediately made her way over and shook Lagos' hand.

"My name is Dr. Eleni Castella. Glad you could make it on such short notice. Our findings are of the utmost importance!"

"Indeed they are," Selim agreed.

He and Eleni looked at each other. Lagos merely smiled at his observation. Perhaps his friend had finally found himself a crush, but he didn't want to get ahead of himself. Clearing his throat, Selim pointed towards the corpse presented on the silver table. Like all deceased, Noah seemed oddly peaceful, as though all burdens of the world had been lifted from his shoulders. The milky white body appeared to have been washed and oiled. Lagos studied the child for a couple of minutes, burning the sight into his mind forever, before inquiring:

"What is this grand discovery of yours?"

"As you can tell by the marks on his throat, Noah was evidently strangled. We are confident that the type of rope used on him was also applied to Kazim."

"How do you know?"

"Both injuries have the same properties in terms of size and structure."

"Could it be a coincidence? Maybe this type of cord is a popular sell in stores."

"Unlikely. We're looking at a material specifically crafted for hunting. We've checked all applicable stores on Milos, and none of them carry it."

"That doesn't mean a local couldn't get his hands on it. One can order anything online these days," Lagos concluded before adding:

"But let's not get too hung up on this just yet. What else can you tell me?"

Dr. Castella stepped forward and explained:

"Noah was first strangled and then thrown into the harbor, just like Kazim. The water levels in his lungs prove our theory."

"The MO is identical, Abi. We have a pattern in these crimes! There's no possibility of multiple predators." Selim had stepped forward and scrutinized his friend once more. Lagos nodded, soaking up all the information.

"Indeed, this boy was also sexually assaulted after he met his tragic end," Dr. Castella confirmed. She was about to say something else when Lagos cut her off.

"What is this?" he asked and pointed out a weird mark around the boy's ankle. He had just noticed it. Dr. Castella replied:

"I was about to tell you. This mark seems to be from a tie of some sort. Perhaps the boy had been bound before death."

"You can't say for certain?"

"No, Detective Inspector."

Lagos' eyes suddenly lit up. Excitedly, he faced Selim and said:

"We need to get to the harbor immediately!"

"Why?"

Selim seemed to be confused by his friend's sudden burst of energy.

"We must talk to Nikos!"

"The fisherman? What for?"

"Two boys with apparent identical MOs are found dead by the port. How come one is missing for an entire week, while the other is found within twenty-four hours after his abduction?"

"I don't know."

"Because one has been there the entire time!"

Selim was confused. Lagos continued explaining:

"Noah has been at the harbor all along, nestled at the depths of the basin where he remained hidden from everyone. It's not the stores that are of relevance to this case, but the water. I bet police divers will find a rock or something heavy with a shredded rope tied around it. Something must've loosened it to the point where Noah was able to float back up to the surface."

"Or perhaps a fish of sorts bit his way through it, and that's why Nikos was only then able to collide with the boy," Selim continued his friend's thought.

It had dawned on him too.

Nikos Zeniades was sitting on the edge of his boat with his feet dangling, eating grapes. When he saw

Lagos and Selim approach, he started waving at them.

"Yassas, detectives! It's good to see you again."

"Likewise, Nikos. We just have a few questions. Mind if we come up?"

"No, not at all. Please, be my guests."

Nikos got up and walked over to help them aboard. Once done, he ushered them to sit down on some pillows before offering them his assortment of fruits.

"What is it you would like to talk about?"

Selim began explaining what he and Dr. Castella had discovered during Noah's autopsy. After finishing, he asked:

"Did you notice rope on the boy's ankle when you pulled him out of the water?"

The fisherman contemplated for a long time, in which he ate multiple dates. Then, he spoke:

"Now that you mention it, the boy did, in fact, have white rope tied around his foot. I apologize for not bringing that up earlier, detectives. I wasn't purposely sabotaging your investigation. I simply wasn't aware of its relevance."

"That is okay, Nikos. We don't always know what might be important later on."

Selim smiled gently at the old man. The fisherman seemed genuinely upset by his faux pas.

"So it's true then! Kazim was not the first victim but the second. He might have witnessed the murderer, thus being collateral damage to something far worse. If Noah hadn't surfaced, there would've never been any connection at all," Lagos concluded after they had gotten off the ship and headed toward his car.

"But why tie Noah to a rock but not Kazim?"

"Because there was no time. Our murderer was simply rushed!"

CLUES

Lagos woke up the next morning feeling hungover.
Connecting Noah's case to Kazim's marked a
significant breakthrough. To properly celebrate
this, he had devoted himself to alcohol, food, and
dirt. After rising from the dead, or what felt like it
at least, he dragged himself into the kitchen and
put the espresso maker on the stove. Turning
around, he looked out into the garden as well as
the city beyond. He noticed a friend of his still
sleeping on the patio lounge. He would have to
wake him up soon, but getting his dose of caffeine
was more important at the moment.

After drinking coffee, taking several
painkillers, and getting under a cold shower, Lagos

felt refreshed enough to tackle the day. The first thing on his agenda was to talk to Paris Markas, the son of Adonis Markas, whom he had met on the day of Noah's discovery at the harbor. During their conversation, Adonis mentioned something about Noah and Paris having been good friends. Perhaps the latter could shed more light on Noah's last couple of hours, given, of course, they had spent the required time together. It was worth a shot, and so Lagos drove out to the coffee shop called 'Demeter' by Lagada Beach.

The coffee shop was a small, wooden building sitting right on the sand. It had surfboards, safety jackets, and starfish hung up on the ceiling. When Lagos stepped in, the place was crawling with customers, most of them happily chatting away. Unsure of where to find Paris, the Detective Inspector decided to walk up to the counter and put in an order. It was there he stumbled upon the person he was looking for. Paris Markas was the spitting image of his father. Handsome beyond average looks or age, the boy had a majestic flow to his every movement. It all seemed so effortless, so smooth. He smiled when Lagos stepped up.

"Yassas. What can I get s-s-started for you today?"

His voice was as rugged as it was innocent. Despite his stutter, he had an outstanding confidence. It made him so captivating he drew all attention without even moving a single muscle. Lagos could tell based on the group of giggling teenage girls sitting nearby. They were all repeatedly throwing furtive glances at him. But Paris seemed completely unfazed by it. The boy was evidently too young to be working here officially. But, as was customary in many places, children helped out in the business of their parents. Especially if the parent is alone.

"Could I get a double shot of espresso, please?"

"Certainly, s-s-sir."

Thanking him, Lagos turned around and found himself a seat. He would wait for the boy to come to him. Not long after, Paris brought over his order.

"You're that detective, right?" Paris asked, looking intricately into Lagos' eyes, "My father s-s-spoke of you the other day."

"You were a friend of Noah's?"

"I was, s-s-sir. I miss him every day."

"Paris, please take a seat for a moment." With that, Lagos motioned the boy to sit down across from him.

"Am I in any sort of trouble?" he asked, still confident but with an air of suspicion.

"Not at all. I'm merely trying to recreate Noah's last few hours before he disappeared. How close were you two?"

"Very close, s-s-sir. I considered him to be one of my best friends. We used to play football together all the time."

Paris' eyes lit up as he spoke. Obviously, the joyful memory had created a warm but somber feeling of nostalgia within him.

"You played on Lagada Beach in your spare time?"

"No, s-s-sir. We used to play for the local football club called 'Islanders'. Noah was our best player, at least according to our head coach," Paris explained.

"What's the coach's name?"

"Emanuel Lorreant. He's a very nice man. We all love him."

Lagos's hunch was confirmed. Mr. Lorreant was, in fact, somehow involved in Noah's life. Finding the child on the doorstep of his most frequently visited club had only been a weak link so far. Now, things looked different. After all, Emanuel was also connected to Kazim in some way. The Detective Inspector was about to formulate his next question when a woman walked in.

Anna Hepburn.

Smiling, she walked over to the counter. There, she patiently waited for someone to take her order.

"Excuse me, Detective. I must attend to the customers," Paris said and got up. After getting behind the counter.

"Yassas Anna. I reckon you're looking for my father?"

"Aren't you a smart boy! Is Adonis around?"

"Yes, he's in the back. I'll go get him for you!"
With that, Paris smiled and turned on his heels.
Anna, in the meantime, let her gaze wander
through the cafe. Hurriedly, Lagos got busy
drinking his coffee, but in reality, he was paying
close attention to their conversation. How come
Anna knew Adonis?

Once the café owner appeared from the
back, the two embraced each other in a heartfelt
hug. Lagos' eyebrows rose more and more by the
minute. She didn't just know him on a customer
basis, she was close to him. As often happens in
crowded spaces, the more people there are, the
louder it becomes. Soon, it grew harder for Lagos
to eavesdrop. In the end, nothing but benign talk
was held unless Dionisis had missed it. As Anna

was about to leave the cafe, the Detective Inspector shot up and went after her.

He caught up to Anna out on the street. She was about to get in her car when he loudly announced her name. Surprised, she turned her head around. When she saw him, all her gaiety from earlier left her face. His mere presence seemed to have evoked the memory of her tragic loss.

"Mrs. Hepburn, what a lovely coincidence it is to find you here today! Got a minute?"

"Sure, just not here. I reckon you want to discuss personal matters but this place has ears for walls. You're welcome to come to my house. I think my husband should be home, too." Lagos agreed and went to his car. After a short drive, the Detective Inspector parked his car in front of the Hepburn's house. As he pulled up, Anna was putting the keys into the front door.

There, she waited for him. Once inside, she offered him a drink, which he accepted. After pouring two negronis, the pair went up on the balcony.

"Didn't you say your husband would be home?"

"Yes, well, I thought he would be. Maybe he had an emergency at work."

She shrugged her shoulders. With sadness on her face, she glanced out into the distance of the light blue sea.

"I couldn't help but notice you being very close with the coffee shop owner."

"Oh, you mean Adonis? Yes, we're good friends."

"How come the two of you know each other?"

Anna eyed the Detective Inspector, evidently trying

to understand the logic behind his questioning. Her reply was unsurprising:

"Why do you care?"

"Adonis Markas was at the scene of your son's discovery. In fact, he was the one to identify him. I'm simply trying to understand Noah's life and the people orbiting it."

"I understand. Well, Adonis and I met during our college days. He had attended Boston University for a study abroad. We got along immediately and dated for a while, too. But, then..."

"Then what?"

"Well, I met Marcus, my husband. I was head over heels for him immediately. So I left Adonis."

"How did Mr. Markas feel about that?"

"He was hurt, of course, but he also understood. After all, it was clear to him that he'd have to return to Greece, and by then, continuing our relationship would've been pointless."

"So you assume he wanted to break things off with you too, sooner or later?"

"Certainly. I mean, Adonis was always very popular with the ladies. I'm sure it was obvious to him that he would find someone new in no time. And that's what he did. Soon after our parting ways, he met Alexandra, with whom he had Paris. They were wildly in love, and since Adonis and I were still friends, we stayed in touch."

"How did Mr. Hepburn feel about this?"

"He never had an issue with him. It was Marcus who suggested to move to Greece in the first place. You see, Detective Inspector, after the housing bubble of '08, he had trouble finding a new job. We opted to leave the country and instead come live here in paradise."

"Adonis never mentioned anything about having a wife. Where could I find her if I wanted to have a word?"

Anna Hepburn remained silent for a moment. Another sad memory had struck her face. Sullenly, she faced the ocean once more.

"Alexandra Markas was a remarkable lady. Energetic and gorgeous. Kind and powerful. But unfortunately, she died giving birth to Paris. Luckily, the boy came out of it unharmed."

"I'm sorry to hear that. Has Mr. Markas since stayed single?"

"Yes. But just now, at the coffee shop, he told me he had found someone new."

Anna's face beamed.

"Who's the new woman?"

"He wouldn't say, wanted to keep it a secret until they go official. I reckon she's beautiful. Our Adonis has fine taste."

Lagos wrote down a couple of words in his notebook. He just had an enlightening thought. Curiously, Anna peered over him. Realizing there was no chance of deciphering his scribbles, she said:

"I hope I'm not kicking you out, Detective Inspector. But I have Pilates in fifteen minutes. So I must ask you to leave now. It's sad going without Noah anymore."

Lagos immediately stopped writing and shot up.

"You took your son to Pilates with you?"

"Oh, yes! I cannot afford a nanny, and Marcus works late sometimes. So I took him along most of the time."

"Mrs. Hepburn, did your son vanish during a Pilates session?"

The seriousness could not have been displayed more clearly on the Detective Inspector's face.

"Yes, how'd you know?"

"A hunch."

"So Adonis has a motive! He knew she would take him to Pilates with her. Perhaps he never got over Anna and, in turn, killed Noah out of jealousy!" Selim said as the two men sat in the dusty Mercedes. Lagos had picked him up from the forensics office after work. As the young Turk slammed his fist on the dashboard, Dionisis didn't reply immediately. He was pondering over the question of who Adonis was currently seeing? Would he really go as far as to kill Anna's son just because he couldn't get over her? Was he still in love with her? And why not kill the husband instead? Why must a child suffer the consequences of an adult's mistakes? How would Adonis benefit from this? Surely, Anna would retreat even more into Marcus's arms and not Adonis's. Unless… it was Marcus who murdered his own child, and Anna knew.

They would have to go back to the Demeter and have a word with Adonis. Maybe he knew more than he led on.

But for now, Lagos and Selim wanted to pay a visit to Emanuel Lorreant first. In one way or another, he was connected to both dead boys. However, the picture was still blurry, so it was time to apply some enhancement filters.

It was a small, run-down house painted in emerald colors. From the outside, the Lorreant house was nothing much to look at. The see-through window by the door had a deep cut running across it and was slightly opened. When Lagos passed by, he peered in but couldn't see anything. There was the smell of apple pie emanating from the inside, so the pair decided to knock anyway. After a few minutes, Amélie opened the door. Her well-groomed mane was tied up in a loose bun, and even with an apron thrown over, she still looked chic. Similar to their first encounter at the boating club, she had a certain air of elegance and sophistication about her. With expressive black eyes, a graceful posture, and a big, perfect smile, she said:

"Detectives! How can I help you?"

"Hello, Mrs. Lorreant. We're looking to have a chat with your husband."

"He's not in at the moment."

Her voice, a melody woven from silk and steel, captivated with tenderness and grace while simultaneously resonating with an underlying strength that commanded attention. Her tone was confident, yet never harsh or overbearing.

"Where can we find him?"

"He's at the boating club. I'm sure you'll find him there, tending to our yacht." Lagos would make an effort to remember her beauty well. He could tell that her mere appearance could stir any place on the island. Perhaps something a certain Adonis Markas didn't pass by unnoticed?

"We'll be sure to follow up on that."

"Is this about Kazim?"

Crossing her arms, Amélie eyed them skeptically.

"It's not just about Kazim anymore. My partner and I are currently investigating the death of two young boys. Your husband has ties to both of them in some..."

"So he's a suspect?"

"We're trying to figure that out. While we're here, would you mind if we asked you some questions too?"

Amélie's unwavering gaze held steady as she extended an invitation for them to come in.

The interior of the house was tidy, with lots of pictures and paintings from either Mrs. or Mr. Lorreant. It was quite contrary to the exterior. Everything was dimmed in dark colors. Stepping inside, they saw that the space opened up with the living room and an adjacent kitchen in the back. To the right were the bedroom, the bathroom, and one door that stood out to Lagos in particular. It was the only crooked, somewhat out-of-place appearing threshold.

"Where does the battered door lead to?" Selim asked, evidently having noticed the same.

"It's the wine cellar, officer."

After offering up coffee, Amélie asked the men to sit down at the dinner table. After helping himself to some sugar, Lagos opened the investigation with:

"What's your profession, Mrs. Lorreant?"

"Call me Amélie. I'm a professor of child psychology at the local university. I've held my chair for the past twelve years."

"What do you like to do in your spare time?"

"I'm an avid saxophone player. Whenever I do end up having some time to myself, I like to spend it on music."

"Does that include the jazz club by the marina?"

"Certainly! My husband and I are regulars there."

"What about your boat? Is that also something you like to do in your time off?"

"The yacht is primarily Emanuel's hobby. We like to have a mix of shared and separate activities. It helps to keep a marriage fit."

"And yet, you do accompany him to the boating club from time to time?"

"Well, yes. Having a boat, even if I don't care much for it, is still an excellent opportunity to get a tan in, right? And it doesn't hurt that a lot of my colleagues from work go there too."

"When's the last time you've been there?"

"A month ago, I'd say."

Lagos and Selim watched as Amélie absentmindedly stirred her coffee, the spoon clinking against the ceramic. She seemed tense, yet every so often, she offered them a small, awkward beam. Selim, who had an appreciation for captivating smiles, leaned in slightly.

"I hope you don't take this the wrong way, but you have a stunning smile."

Amélie chuckled. "Thank you, officer. It wasn't always like that, though. As a kid, I had incredibly crooked teeth. Then I had a nasty skateboard accident where I hit my face on a curb and knocked out my upper central incisor tooth. After that, I had braces for years, but in the end, they were useless. The damage was too severe, and my second incisors turned blue before falling out completely. Eventually, they replaced them altogether. Honestly, that stage of my life was awful. The other kids never let me hear the end of it. But I guess that's just the cruelty of honest children, right?"

"I'm sorry you had to go through that," Selim said. He had been bullied occasionally at school too as a child, so he understood her well. After asking some more questions, the team understood that there was nothing more to be gained from the conversation. So, they decided to leave. As it had gotten rather late, the two of them headed home instead of paying Emanuel Lorreant a visit at the boating club.

Something they would regret bitterly the next day.

ANOTHER MISSING CHILD

Lagos and Selim sat across from one another, both preoccupied with their scrambled eggs and orange juice. The sun had risen roughly an hour ago, and it was already getting considerably warm. While Selim got up to help himself to another serving, Lagos was pulled out of smoking his drift when the telephone rang. After walking over and picking it up, he heard an officer from the police station address him on an urgent matter.

"Another boy has gone missing. The report just came in."

"Who?"

For reasons unknown, Lagos felt like he knew the

answer already. With a grim visage, he waited for a reply.

"Paris Markas."

No less than fifteen minutes later, Lagos and Selim left the mansion. Understanding that so far, all fingers pointed towards Emanuel Lorreant as being the predator, Lagos wanted to drive over to the local university. Amélie Lorreant was most likely the only person who knew exactly where to find her husband. They would have to hurry, though. Both Lagos and Selim were painfully aware that Paris could be killed any minute.

If he wasn't already.

Not long after, the dusty Mercedes pulled into the parking lot. Hurriedly, the detectives got out and made their way over to Amélie's office. They knew where to find her, thanks to last night's informal interrogation. When they knocked on her door, they could hear her say:

"Come in."

Amélie Lorreant sat behind a maroon-colored wooden desk. Papers lay scattered across her workspace. She was immersed in some file when the two men entered. Looking up, she smiled.

"I was wondering when you'd come to see me. I just didn't expect it to be so soon."

"Where's your husband right now?"

Instead of replying, Mrs. Lorreant merely raised a finger and pointed it past the two of them. Simultaneously looking back, Lagos and Selim faced Emanuel Lorreant standing in the doorway.

"What's this about?" Emanuel asked, clearly confused by the tension in the room.

"We must talk, Mr. Lorreant!"

Selim had stepped forward. Emanuel complied but wanted to ask his wife something first. Granting his wish, the two policemen remained glued to their spot.

"Amélie, Mon Amour, I just wanted to check if you're having your therapy sessions today?"

"Well, of course I am, Mon Coeur."

With a nod, Mr. Lorreant motioned the detectives to follow him out. He didn't want his wife to be part of the inevitable conversation they were about to have. However, only Lagos followed. Selim purposely stayed back with Amélie. There was something he needed to know.

Once outside, Emanuel started walking down the corridor and up some stairs.

"Where exactly are we going?" Lagos asked suspiciously.

"To my office."

"Pardon?"

"Detective Inspector, I am a professor of advanced mathematics at this pristine college. I hold a chair and subsequently have my own office." After entering his office, Emanuel asked Lagos to sit down.

"Mr. Lorreant, you are aware of the children who have gone missing lately?"

"How very straightforward you are, Detective Inspector."

Emanuel handed Lagos a cup of black tea. After taking a seat himself, he examined his opposite keenly.

"I have no time to waste," Lagos replied coolly.

"Oh, I'm sure you don't."

"Answer my question then!"

"Last I heard, young Kazim was found murdered by the harbor. A tragic loss, indeed. But, I only know about this because you came to talk to me about it at the boating club."

"Do you know a boy called Noah Hepburn?"

"Perhaps."

"What about Paris Markas? Does that ring a bell?"

"No."

"But you have heard of Noah Hepburn's murder? Or the most recent vanishing of Paris Markas?"

Even though Lagos' eyes burned themselves through Emanuel's skin and inward to peek at the very core of his being, the latter remained as calm as ever. He replied:

"This is the first time I've heard about this."

"Is it? Then explain to me this: You claim to have never heard of any of those boys or their tragic fates, and yet you have at least one touching point with each child, murdered or missing."

"Are you insinuating I had something to do with it?"

"Your vagueness certainly doesn't help me think otherwise."

"Well, Monsieur, I can only attest to my innocence. I swear, I had nothing to do with any of it! Now, if you'll excuse me, I must get back to work. Be so kind as to close the door on your way out, yes?"

Meanwhile, Selim sat across from Amélie Lorreant. He requested to view the list of clients requiring therapy. As he skimmed through the pages, he asked her:

"What type of work do you provide?"

"I move in the field of logopedics. In other words, speech therapy. I help children who suffer from reading disorders and the like. Have you heard of dyslexia before?"

"Yes. I struggled with that too as a young boy."

Understandingly, Amélie nodded. Selim continued sifting through the files until he stumbled upon a name that made him stop dead in his tracks.

Paris Markas.

POWER MOVES

After leaving the university grounds, Lagos and Selim headed over to the Demeter. It was as busy as usual. When the two of them entered, Adonis Markas was in the process of making a cold brew.

"Welcome in, officers! What're you having today?"

"Two espressos and some answers would be fantastic."

Adonis' face turned grim. He had most likely anticipated his interrogation. He explained to them that he would have to finish up some orders but would meet them out on the beach later. When the pair stepped outside, the golden sand lay glittering under the setting sun. Colors of orange, yellow, and pink began to burst from the sky. Thin, white clouds wandered across the firmament. Both Lagos and Selim each lit a cigarette as they took in the scene. Not long after, Adonis joined them.

"Walk with me," he invited.

Silently, the men obliged before starting off towards the east. Lagos asked:

"Tell us about Paris' last movements. When did you see him last?"

"We were working in the coffee shop. It was even busier than usual. Suddenly, I realized he was running late for his therapy session. So, I told him to scurry along. He didn't come home after that. At first, I thought he might've planned to meet up with friends or something. When night fell, I was certain something was terribly wrong. Something my gut had been telling me for hours at that point."

"What kind of therapy was he undergoing?"

"He was in treatment for dyslexia."

"Where did these sessions take place?"

"At university. He was seeing Dr. Lorreant."

"Do you reckon he could've been snatched on his way to or from the session?"

It was Selim who had posed the question. Adonis could tell by his face that the answer was of utmost importance to the man. So he truthfully replied:

"I don't know."

As they walked past a grove of palm trees, Adonis was on the verge of tears. His body was trembling as though stricken by a terrible plague. His eyes had dark rings around them. It was obvious he was sleep-deprived.

"I will never forget his smile as he waved me goodbye. Oh god, I just want him to come home."

As the men returned to the coffee shop, Lagos inquired about Adonis' newfound relationship with the mysterious woman. Initially, he hesitated to disclose her identity. Appalled by Lagos' inquiry, he asked how they had heard about it in the first place. Lagos refused to give away the name and instead implored him to reveal the mystery woman's identity.

"Whoever you're currently seeing might be the reason for Paris' abduction. We need to know!"

"Let me show you something," Adonis sighed. He led them into the back room. It was dimly lit and smelled of coffee beans. There, he started to rummage in some stack of papers until he produced a battered-looking letter. "Read this! You'll understand."

Dear Emanuel,

I hope this letter finds you well. It's not easy for me to write this, but it is more necessary now than ever. After a lot of soul-searching lately, I've come to the realization that I'm not comfortable with the direction our relationship has taken.

Starting off by affirming that my feelings for you are genuine, our time together holds significant meaning. However, honesty dictates a harsh truth— I am not bound to the same constellation as you, my love. While feeling a strong attraction towards you, it's been confusing for me to navigate. Sorry if I've led you on in any way.

We've shared some intimate moments, and I cherish those memories. But our entanglement cannot continue, knowing that it's not true to who I am. The thought of what people might think if they found out about us is terrifying. The consequences it could have on both of us, particularly if your wife finds out, haunt me at night. The mere thought of it!

Please know that this decision doesn't diminish the special place you hold in my heart. You've brought joy and warmth into my mundane existence, and I will always be grateful for that. But for the sake of our own well-being, we should part ways now.

Hopefully, you can understand where all of this is coming from and that you can find it within you to forgive me one day.

Take care of yourself, Emanuel. I wish you nothing but happiness and fulfillment in your future.

Love,

Your Adonis

"Has Emanuel seen this already?" Lagos asked sternly. Adonis nodded, before adding:

"This is a copy for safekeeping. I put the original in his mailbox roughly a week ago."

"How did he react to it?"

"I have no idea. He never got back to me."

"Not in the best way, then," Selim chuckled. His smirk quickly faded when he saw Adonis' disapproving glare. Lagos knew they would have to confront Emanuel Lorreant about this in one way or the other. The Detective Inspector thus diverted the conversation to another topic. One last subject he had to address.

"You know a woman named Anna Hepburn, right?"

"Annie? Of course! We met back in college."

"And you were sweethearts for a while, yes?"

Adonis immediately blushed. He asked, rather defensively:

"What's this got to do with anything?"

"Is she the reason you couldn't commit to Emanuel Lorreant?"

"You're joking, right? Of course not! I explained it in the letter, I don't swing the other way. Simple as that."

"And yet, you led Mr. Lorreant on! Knowing, as you put it, 'that you're with none of that'! Come on now, Adonis, you're no mere experimenting teenager anymore. What's the real reason for your breaking up with Emanuel?"

Adonis looked like a cornered animal. He was fuming and seriously debated to slap the Detective Inspector across the face for his rather insulting pressuring tactics. But then, he dropped his shoulders and confessed:

"Yes, it's true. She had broken up with me over Marcus. At first, I thought I could move on by drowning my feelings in sex and drugs. But, whenever I was on my own, the feelings came creeping back. Then, I met my wife, Alexandra. The emotional state was stable for so long that I was convinced I had finally come to terms with it. But then... my poor Alex, I loved her so much. Death took her from me when Paris was born. And just like that, the feelings for Annie came back. It didn't help that she and her now husband, this prick, had moved to Milos in the meantime."

"So you murdered Noah to take revenge on her for choosing another man? For the simple reason of never having moved on?"

"No, never! I flung myself into an affair with Emanuel. But it didn't work. It simply felt off. And even if I was still in love with Annie, your accusation is still nonsense! If I had actually committed this crime, would I then murder my own son?"

"Who said anything about there only being one killer?"

Adonis Markas suddenly went quiet. He seemed embarrassed as if he had just let slip a piece of information that wasn't supposed to be revealed.

Selim's smirk had reappeared.

Not long after, the Detective Inspector and his companion left the coffee shop. Lagos had brutally continued grinding Adonis to the point where the latter started to cry.

"So Emanuel Lorreant and Adonis Markas had an affair. One broke things off, the other didn't take it well. In the ensuing heartache, Emanuel takes revenge on Adonis by kidnapping his son?" Selim wondered before hurriedly adding:

"Or, a completely different scenario: Adonis kidnaps and murders Noah Hepburn. His motive? Anna Hepburn's breaking up with him back in college. Evidently, he hasn't gotten over it yet. After the deed was done, Anna and Marcus find out what he had done and now retaliate by letting Paris disappear?"

"No. Where would that put Kazim? Something is off. I just can't put my finger on it. We're clearly missing a piece to this puzzle."

"What about Emanuel Lorreant? He could've snatched Paris at the therapy session. He knew from his wife about the location and time of each client."

"Yes, we need to talk to Mr. Lorreant again. But it'll have to wait until tomorrow. There is something else I must do first."

For some, the next day brought paradise-like living conditions, for others, hell on earth. Lagos and Selim were knocking on Adonis Markas' door once more. With frizzy hair and crusty eye sockets, the coffee shop owner opened up to them. Yawning, he asked if they had come back to torment him with more questioning.

"Would you mind accompanying us? We need your help," Selim explained and motioned him to get in the dusty Mercedes. Call it a parent's instinct or pure animal cunning, but Adonis' immediate sense of fear and suspicion made it clearly obvious that he knew what this was all about. He started whimpering:

"Please, no! Don't do this to me."

No response.

Instead, Lagos opened the backseat door. Tears started falling down Adonis' cheeks. The man knew there was no way out, so he complied and got in. The car drove back into the city before turning towards the harbor. With every second passing, Adonis started trembling more. A small crowd of onlookers had started to gather by the docking stations. Once as close as they could get, Lagos got out of his car, walked around, and opened the door for the parent. Facing the crowd, he shouted: "Get out of here! Have you nothing better to do?" Embarrassed by their own curiosity people made way. As Lagos walked ahead briskly, Adonis followed. Some of the people who did not immediately comply with the Detective Inspector's demand to leave scurried away last minute so they could walk on by. Right by the cornerstones of the docking station, Dionisis stepped aside. Adonis walked up and glanced down into the water.

There he was.

Face down, floating on his stomach, whipped by the waves, was Paris Markas. His son. Adonis fell to his knees, clutching the stones beneath him with crushing desperation. Tears cascaded down his face, and then, from the depths of his soul, he let out a cry so hauntingly mournful it stirred even the gods. Selim, unmoved, kept his hands buried deep in his pockets. He could not look upon the man, for he was holding back his own sorrow. In an attempt to acknowledge the devastation of it all, Lagos bowed his head. It might have been his way of fighting back his own cries, too. In his thoughts, he cursed himself for not arresting the killer quick enough. But he also knew that this case was still purely circumstantial. He wasn't any closer to catching the perpetrator than he was when they had found Kazim. At this point, an arrest simply wasn't feasible. His hands were tied.

"You killed my boy... You were meant to protect the people of this island, and now my son paid the ultimate price for your incompetence. This is on you, don't you ever forget it."

It was a mere whisper, and even though Adonis hadn't moved a single muscle, Lagos knew he was being rebuked.

"You're right! And there's absolutely nothing I can do about it now. I'm sorry for letting you down, Adonis. Hopefully, one day you'll find it in your heart to forgive me," Dionisis said, sadness swaying in his voice.

He turned and walked off.

Later that afternoon, after turning sorrow into belligerence with endless thoughts of failure, an espresso, and a big drift of dirt, Lagos and Selim made their way to the boating club. After entering and walking up to the counter, they asked the bartender if Emanuel Lorreant had been in. The man explained that Lorreant had just left to do some work on his yacht but that they could find him out there. So, they went looking for him, and indeed, a topless, sweaty Emanuel was tying a knot around one of the back pillars.

"Afternoon, officers! Wonderful day out, eh?"

"Depends on who you ask. We do have a couple questions that we'd love for you to answer."

"Sure, why don't you come up? Join me for this fresh batch of dirty martinis I just made." A couple of minutes later, the two officers sat on the finest leather seats, looking at Emanuel, wiping the sweat off his face with a white towel. He then handed each of them a glass of liquor. He smiled enthusiastically as he said:

"Like I said, freshly made."

"Is that a hobby of yours? The art of cocktails?"

"I'm sure you haven't come here to ask me about my hobbies. This isn't a first date."

Emanuel laughed heartedly.

"What do you think we've come to ask you?"

"Not a clue in the world."

"Did you also serve Adonis Markas a dirty martini on your first date?"

The laughing stopped immediately. Where joy had resided in his face just a moment ago, now started to appear seriousness and resentment.

"How'd you know about this?"

"Was it on this yacht, too, where you gave yourself to him for the first time?"

"You are way out of line, Inspector!"

"It's Detective Inspector to you, and no, I don't think so, Mr. Lorreant! I think this might just be the reason why young Paris had to lose his life! You were, and still are, madly in love with Adonis Markas, isn't it so?"

"Not true."

Lagos ignored him and continued hammering him with accusations.

"His breaking up with you may have unhinged you just enough to kidnap and murder his son in an act of brutal revenge!"

"No!"

"You raped Paris because taking him from his father wasn't enough gratification!"

"Shut up!"

Emanuel shouted. The two men stared each other down intently. Finally, Lorreant broke the silence.

"Okay. You're right, Detective Inspector! I am in love with Adonis. And we did have a relationship, one which he just recently broke off. But I am no psychopath! I would never harm his boy. I loved Paris as much as I did his father! You must believe me!"

Lagos let himself fall back on the cushions. Visibly irritated, he massaged his temples. Selim, watching his friend, understood that he had let off steam from the tensions of the morning.

"Tell me everything," Lagos demanded, now calm as ever.

"My wife, Amélie, had found out about my affair with Adonis. We had to break things off soon anyway. It was a foolish thing to do. But, Detective Inspector, have you ever been so madly in love that you couldn't imagine being without the other person?"

Sometime later, Lagos and Selim went back into the boating club. The Detective Inspector wanted to request another drink after the bar on Emanuel's yacht had run out. The bartender was in the process of making a whiskey sour when Selim pointed out:

"There it is again. This odd smell."

Lagos noticed it, too, now. It was an odor he knew only too well. Like bloodhounds, they started sniffing around the place until they ended up in front of the door leading down to the basement.

"You can't go down there!" Emanuel Lorreant protested. He had just walked in from the outside. He rushed in front of the door and protectively put up his arms wide.

"And why is that?" Selim returned.

"It's employees and members only."

"We are the police! Now make way!"

In his defeat, he stepped aside once Selim threatened to punch his teeth in. All three of them went down and came across something none of the officers had expected.

It appeared to be a smuggler's storage. An entire room, its windows taped down with black plastic, was decked out with fishing gear and nautical equipment. Illegal motor parts hung from the ceiling with white rope. Or at least, that's what should have been there, because roughly two-thirds of it was gone.

"Who's storing illegal equipment down here?" Lagos demanded to know, "Is this some sort of passive income for the club?"

"No. It's mine," Emanuel admitted.

"Are you running a black market down here?"

"No, I'm just a collector. But in my defense, all of it was stolen recently!"

Lagos and Selim looked at each other first before consecutively scrutinizing Emanuel.

"What do you mean it was stolen?" Lagos reiterated.

"I don't know. I didn't tell anyone about this gear shed. Not a single word. And then, one morning, I walked in here to check on my latest arrivals to find them all gone. Nothing but the hanging ropes remaining."

"Who knew about this black dock?" Selim asked.

"I have a hunch," Lagos realized grimly.

He had finally connected a dot. One that had been bothering him from the beginning.

REVELATIONS

Dionisis Lagos and Selim parked in front of the Yavuz house. A couple minutes earlier, the latter had called his cousin Hakan to see if the family was in. After a knock, Aylin appeared at the door. She smiled when she saw them. She seemed to have improved since the last time they visited her. Something that put Lagos at ease. It was beyond imagination to lose one's own child, but it showed true strength of character to come to terms with it. Aylin welcomed them in and immediately offered freshly made kunefe and black tea. Right as they accepted the offer, Murat Yavuz stepped down the stairs. With a hot cup of tea in his hand, Lagos announced,

"Ah yes, the man we've been looking for in the first place. Come, Murat, sit down. Please."

"What's this about, uncle?"

Murat looked pleadingly at Selim. The latter didn't speak up immediately before asking:

"How did you get your hands on the boat parts?"

"I'm not following."

"When we came here last, you were arguing with your father about consuming dirt. Back then, you told us that you had it from a friend. But that was a lie, wasn't it?"

"No!"

"Yes, it was!"

"Prove it then!"

"The empty basement at the boating club! You took it all!"

Selim was furious. Being lied to by his own family deeply upset him. Lagos was casually sipping on his black tea. Hakan and Aylin walked into the living room as Murat confessed:

"I knew you'd find out sooner or later. It's true, the money isn't from a well-paying job. I also lied about the dirt. It isn't from a friend. I was afraid you'd put me in jail for what I did, that's why I went and sold the illegal boating equipment to buy myself some drugs. But there's also another reason I haven't told you sooner."

Murat now looked at his parents, who seemed like they were about to murder him with their eyes.

"You robbed the place together with Kazim, didn't you?"

Lagos had spoken while simultaneously putting down his empty tea cup on the glass table beside his chair.

"Yes. I once visited my brother at work. He had forgotten to pack his lunch, so Anne asked me to drop it off. When I walked into that place, I identified the petrol smell of the boating parts immediately and wondered if something illegal was going on in here. It was odd for the indoor of a boating club to smell like that. After handing over the lunchbox to Kazim, I went on a little exploration walk, and sure enough, I found myself down in the basement. What I saw blew my mind. Meters upon meters of diving equipment, fishing gear, and boat parts. It was a black-market dock! I could tell by the way some of the motors were modified, that someone knew what they were doing down there. After I left and Kazim returned from work, I confronted him about it. He swore never having heard of it before. My brother was too young to understand the appeal of it all. But still, when I hacked out a plan to loot the basement, he was eager to help. And that's what we did. We went there and cleared it out. Kazim stayed back to stand guard while I took care of loading the stuff into my car. The idea was that I would return on my own, like the sunshine at dawn, to drive it off somewhere safe. It all went well until we made our way home."

"He had been spooked by something," Lagos interjected, observing the young man closely.

"Yes! He was completely freaked out. I thought he was just shaken from the theft. You know, too much adrenalin rushing through his body."

"So he witnessed something?"

"Maybe! He kept talking about shadows. I thought he was just scared of the dark."

"He wasn't. He had witnessed the murder of Noah Hepburn. He had seen the killer! The same person who followed you home. The phantom that snatched him from his bed," Lagos concluded.

"How horrible! My poor boy," Aylin stammered. She had teared up a little.

"It must've been someone with a familiar face. One Kazim would recognize and trust. Perhaps, when the killer knocked on his window that night, he didn't even connect it to your little heist," Lagos murmured, brainstorming.

"I know just the person," Selim said and looked at the Detective Inspector meaningfully. The latter nodded.

"I'm sorry for not coming forward with this story sooner. I feel like I caused my brother's death. It's still so hard to talk about these things," Murat explained, and a single tear fell from his cheek.

In the evening, Lagos and Selim went to visit Anna Hepburn during her Pilates session. The lesson took place on the second floor of some rusty, old building. Considering its size, it must've been a factory back in the day. Patiently, the men waited on the stairs that led up to the class. They could hear a female trainer giving instructions inside. Selim was rolling a cigarette, leaning against the railing, when Anna came out. She wore a towel around her neck and had a pink mat clutched under her left armpit.

"Hello, officers," she breathed.

"Yassas, Mrs. Hepburn. How was your workout?" Lagos asked. Meanwhile, Selim lit his cigarette and let out a big cloud of smoke. Anna replied that it went well. Lagos was about to speak when another person appeared from inside the room, leaving both men star-struck.

Amélie Lorreant.

Sweaty but still stunning to look at, she made her way down to them. The look she gave both detectives now was a far cry from the one they had received during their conversation in her office.

"Are you gentlemen interested in taking up some lessons? It would certainly do you good," Amélie chuckled.

"You never mentioned Pilates before."

"A woman should always have her secrets."

"Has your husband ever attended any classes here?" Selim inquired and let out a final puff before stomping the bud on the ground.

"No, why should he? He's busy doing other types of sports, if you get my twist," Amélie returned, sounding hurt, "Have a pleasant evening, gentlemen."

Mrs. Lorreant walked past them but made sure to give Selim one last lingering look.

"I think Emanuel and she are not on the best terms right now," Anna remarked behind her hand.

"Clearly," Selim added while looking after Mrs. Lorreant, who had just reached her car.

"What did you want to talk to me about, officers?"

"Evidently, Amélie's husband never attended any classes. But has he ever dropped his wife off here?"

"Sometimes."

With that answer, the officers thanked Anna for her time and let her go. As the woman approached her vehicle, Lagos addressed Selim by asking:

"What's your take on this?"

"The killer knew Noah would accompany his mother to Pilates. This is where they snatched him."

The two were pulled out of their brainstorming session when a shabby-looking man in a grey overall called out to them from around the corner. It was the janitor.

"Gentlemen, I overheard you talking, and I might have some information for you."

THIRD TIME'S THE CHARM

Dionisis Lagos spent the next few days at home, brooding over the case. He could be seen trawling about the entire house. Meanwhile, Selim assisted the forensics office with his knowledge. Lagos was in the process of drying himself off after going for a swim in his outdoor pool when the landline rang.

"Merhaba, Abi. The examination of Paris' body has been completed. Can you come by? Right now?"

"On my way."

The two men looked upon the nudity of Paris Markas. He, too, was now pale and pasty-looking. The more dead bodies Lagos got to see, the less human they appeared to him. It was almost unfathomable that only a couple of days ago, this very boy right here had been serving him coffee and now lay on this table, silent for eternity.

"The reports show a consistent pattern with prior victims. Paris Markas was suffocated, sexually assaulted, and then thrown into the sea," Selim explained while reading off the documents.

"He was dressed nicely, too, when we found him," Lagos noted casually.

"Indeed. But there is one crucial difference between Kazim and Noah. We're unsure of the murderer's intention, but Paris is missing an upper central incisor tooth. Or rather, the one inside his mouth is a fake! The original has been surgically removed. From what we can tell, it was done by someone who knew what they were doing."

"Have you checked the previous victims?"

"Not yet. That's what I wanted you here for."

Lagos and Selim looked each other in the eyes. Once again, their brotherly connection aligned their thought patterns. If Kazim and Noah were, in fact, missing an upper central incisor tooth, then this would mean the murderer was a collector of sorts. A revelation crucial to finding the demon haunting this island. Lagos ordered with a faint voice:

"Bring out the bodies."

The tension was so thick it could almost be grabbed out of the air as the bodies of Kazim and Noah were retrieved from the cooler. They were placed on metallic tables right next to Paris. It was the first time all three victims lay in the same room. It was an odd thought Lagos had as he observed them — Brothers united in death. This time around, it was the Detective Inspector who glanced over Selim's shoulder. His heart was pounding out of his chest as he awaited his friend's conclusion. While Selim shed a flashlight into Kazim's mouth, he determined:

"Missing a front tooth."

Silently, they went over to Noah's body, where Selim quickly opened the mouth and soon after exclaimed:

"Prothesis!"

There it was. The killer was a collector of teeth. And even though this felt like a success of sorts, Lagos was beyond frustrated.

"God! How did we not notice this before?"

TO PINPOINT A MURDERER

The air was stiff. The room was messy. No one had cleaned in days. It was far from the image she usually gave off. Amélie Lorreant seemed all dirty and distraught during her chat with Lagos and Selim. The two had been sitting across from her for the past thirty minutes. Occasionally, she had cried. White streaks were noticeable around her eyes. Her hands kept wringing with each other.

"He's a dirty cheater. A dog! How could he do this to me?"

"Where's he now, Amélie?"

"In the depths of hell, I hope."

Lagos' eyes lowered to the floor, fixating on the Turkish rug. He sighed.

"I loved him! And then he goes out to bang this man-whore running his little coffee shop down by the beach."

"How did you find out about Emanuel and Adonis, Mrs. Lorreant?" Selim asked.

"Don't call me by his last name! How insensitive of you."

"Amélie…"

"Well, it was obvious. A woman, no, in fact, all humans feel it in their guts when their significant other is slipping away. When they emotionally retreat and move on. It's one of the most painful things in the world. I could tell that Emanuel was going through something, but whenever I tried talking about it, he blocked me off. Then, he started working late, would go out to the boating club more frequently, and so forth. I simply connected the dots."

"Did he eventually confess?"

"Of course not! I found a letter in the mailbox from an unknown sender. There was no address or name on the envelope, so I opened it and started reading. It was from Adonis Markas, breaking things off with my ... with Emanuel."

"Did you confront him about this?"

"No, not at first. I wanted to see if he had the guts to tell me himself, now that things were over. But he never mentioned a single word. He didn't even cry. To make sure this wasn't my imagination playing tricks on me, I went through Emanuel's phone. And sure enough, there were hundreds of photos with Adonis, all stacked away in a separate folder called 'Mon Petit Saint.' After that, I went and talked to him about it. It ended in a huge argument."

"Does he come home at all?"

"Sometimes. I reckon he sleeps a lot in his office."

"I understand."

"You know, officers, the worst thing about it is that, at first, I thought he was cheating on me with a woman. For reasons I cannot explain, his being with another man hurts even more. It just makes me wonder if he was ever even attracted to me at all."

"Are you thinking of Anna Hepburn?" Lagos suddenly intervened. He had reappeared from his slumber.

"How'd you know? I suppose it doesn't matter. You are the great Detective Inspector, after all. Either way, the answer is yes. Once I had my suspicions about Emanuel, I occasionally followed him around. I was curious to know where he went. He frequented the Demeter. So many times did I watch him talk to Adonis and Anna there. I was

certain she was the one who held his heart."
While Selim asked what she planned on doing now,
Lagos excused himself for the bathroom. Amélie,
while explaining that she was considering a
divorce, pointed to the right. The Detective
Inspector silently raised himself and walked off. On
his way to the bathroom, Lagos suddenly noticed
the door to the cellar being open. Not thinking
about it twice, he decided to take a little detour.

The basement was musty and dark. The
only light available came from a tiny window on the
top right. There were at least a half dozen wine
racks. Lagos also noticed plenty of cobwebs around
the corners of the shelves. Not quite sure what he
was looking for, he started to wander along the
different pieces of furniture. Once reaching the
back end of the room, Lagos discovered a small
wooden desk. Normally, he wouldn't have paid

much attention to it. But this was different. Unlike the rest down here, this piece of furniture looked freshly cleaned. Someone had used it recently. Pausing briefly to hear if anyone was coming, Lagos started to casually inspect the desk in further detail. Different documents and pencils were lying around. The middle drawer held a couple of photo albums of Emanuel and Amélie. It was the last compartment that caught Lagos off guard. A heavy lock kept it shut. Like a sniffer dog zeroing in on a scent, Dionisis had to know what was hidden inside. The Detective Inspector looked around and found himself a large hammer. Praying not to be heard by Amélie upstairs, he let the tool fall upon the latch. Once, twice, thrice, before it broke into two pieces and fell to the ground. Swiping the sweat off his forehead, Lagos knelt down and pulled heavily on the last compartment. What he discovered astonished him:

A revolver, some white rope, and a surgical knife.

The gun was a Smith & Wesson Model 29, frequently called a 'Dirty Harry'. It was the most common firearm for civilians on Milos, the ideal weapon to have someone do one's bidding. The surgical knife would have to be checked for DNA, but Lagos had no doubt in his mind that this was the tool with which the incisor teeth of the victims had been removed. What Lagos found interesting even more was the white rope. It was the one from the basement of the boating club. But not just that, it was the type specifically designed for hunting. This was the proof they had been looking for all this time. In his mind, the Detective Inspector had caught his killer.

Later that day, Lagos returned to his mansion on the hill. He had practically solved this case. It was evident who the murderer was. All things pointed towards one person. The rope and knife in their basement certainly didn't help them get rid of the skeletons in their closet. "But what was the motive?" Lagos asked himself out loud as he poured himself a whiskey sour.

"Let's think this through: Noah Hepburn, the first victim, gets kidnapped during a Pilates workout. Something the killer knew because they frequently dropped off their significant other for the lessons. I'm sure they had noticed the boy and vice versa. After having their way with the poor soul, the murderer sunk the body in the harbor. But, in the process of doing so, they are observed by Kazim. Kazim was standing guard while his brother raided the basement of the boating club.

With their cover blown, the murderer trails the boys back home. There, they snatch Kazim out of his own bed before leaving him for dead at the port. The last victim, Paris, is taken on his way to or from his therapy session with Amélie. Something the killer was aware of, as they had access to the professor's calendar. But why? Why kill Noah in the first place? Why kill Paris after the whole island was already on high alert from Noah and Kazim's discovery?"

As the last few words still rang in his head, Lagos downed his entire glass before making himself a new drink. Refueled, the brooding man went across his living room and out into the gardens. The sun had settled a couple of hours ago, so now the whole of Adamantas shown out into the night in a ray of golden and silver lights.

"What if the motive for the crimes weren't sexually driven? Perhaps there are multiple reasons why those three boys were murdered," Lagos continued to speak to himself,

"Clearly, Emanuel's a creep, so perhaps he found Noah attractive and couldn't resist his urges any longer? Would that mean he was infatuated with Paris, too?"

OF DEEPLY BURIED SECRETS

Lagos and Selim walked along under the prominent oak trees of the university. Both wore long, black overcoats to protect themselves from the light rain and wind. They were on their way to talk to Amélie Lorreant. Her husband hadn't answered any of their calls, and he was neither at his office nor the boating club. Understanding the gravity of his situation, he most likely fled to some remote location. The man would either turn up by himself or be found through a manhunt. It all came down to whether Amélie would willingly surrender the evidence from her cellar or if the officers had to obtain a search warrant first. Lagos had a feeling Amélie would be more than willing to give up any incriminating evidence against her defamatory husband. Additionally, Lagos wanted to learn more about Emanuel's past and his marriage in general.

Lagos and Selim were approaching Professor Lorreant's office, casually talking about grabbing moussaka after this, when one of them suddenly motioned for the other to be silent. From inside the office, loud angry voices could be heard. The officers silently crept up all the way to the slightly opened door and listened in.

"I demand answers, Professor Lorreant! You've violated my son's trust and his integrity with your despicable actions!"
It was a woman, roughly in her late forties, who had spoken. Amélie Lorreant returned, equally heated:

"Excuse me? How dare you make such baseless accusations! I am a respected professional at this university. I would never engage in such misconduct!"

"Respected professional? Do you call preying on vulnerable children professionalism? My son trusted you, confided in you, and you took advantage of him!"

"Your allegations are outrageous and unfounded! I've dedicated my life to helping young minds navigate their struggles. I've never crossed any boundaries, certainly not with your son!" The mother scoffed loudly, putting her hands on her hips, before shouting:

"Don't you dare deny it! He came home from your therapy session acting differently, avoiding eye contact, and with a sense of shame he never had before. You've scarred him for life!"

"You have no evidence, just baseless accusations fueled by your own hysteria. I demand an apology for this slander!"

"An apology? I'll see you in court, Malaka! I'll make sure everyone knows what kind of demon you really are. You can't hide behind your masquerade forever."

"What a preposterous way of assassinating my character. I am done talking to you. Leave my office, now!"

Lagos and Selim had heard enough. Before either of the women had a chance to notice them, the two left. The Detective Inspector just had a profound revelation. As if someone had lifted a veil from his eyes. There was no need to talk to Amélie anymore. To anyone, in fact.

It was time to do some research.

Lagos and Selim pretty much burst through the entrance of the police station. Some of the officers filling out paperwork looked at them in confusion.

"We must get access to the archives immediately!" Lagos ordered. The poor receptionist hadn't even managed to ask what they were looking for.

He glanced at them unbothered, his eyes scanning the two men from head to toe. After a brief moment of contemplation, he gestured toward the hallway. Chewing his gum obnoxiously loud, the man said:

"Archive's down this way, last door to your right."

Without thanking him, Lagos and Selim started walking down the floor. On either side, there were prison cells. Once reaching the last compartment, the Detective Inspector suddenly stopped.

Someone had addressed him.

"If it isn't the renowned Inspector Lagos."

At first, he didn't see the person talking. Only after they had stepped out of the shadows did he see that it was a woman. Lagos blinked a couple times before recognizing who was facing him:

Helena Kostea.

She looked ragged, with sunken eyes, frizzy hair, and hollow cheekbones. By the looks of it, she hadn't eaten in days. The once most beautiful woman on the entire island had fallen deep. Lagos told her so. She merely scoffed at him.

"By the way, it's Detective Inspector now."

"Well, would you look at that! Glad I could bring you to fame and glory. How's my lover doing?"

"Joey's dead. I suppose losing everything and being betrayed by the one you care about most can eventually break a man. He took his own life months ago."

Helena retreated into the dark. Lagos knew she was trying to hide her tears. A moment passed before she found her words again.

"How awful! When was the funeral?"

"No clue," Lagos said truthfully before adding:

"I'm sorry for what happened to you. I can't possibly imagine what it feels like to bear all this guilt. But, if it makes you feel any better, Stefanie Sigmund still haunts my every dream too. It feels profoundly unjust that someone else had to lose their life for me to gain all these riches and titles. A sadness I cannot shake anymore. If I could rewind time and prevent it all, I'd do it in a heartbeat, even if it meant to give up everything."

Silence.

"I appreciate that, Detective Inspector."

With that, Lagos turned and walked off. Selim smiled at him.

After descending the stairs to the archives, the officers came upon countless registries containing a file on every single Melian inhabitant. It was like trying to find a needle in a haystack. But they had to give it a shot. Surprisingly quick, they came across the file cabinet containing names starting with "L." After sifting through some of the yellow papers, they found what they were looking for:

'Lorreant Amélie'.

Selim opened the file and started to skim the different entries, Lagos doing the same alongside him. Barely a minute into reading, Selim whispered: "This is bad, Abi. Real bad."

"Yeah, we need to hurry!"

DIRTY HARRY

The Lorreant house was packed to the brim. Amélie Lorreant stood in the kitchen, leaning on the countertop facing the living room. She waited for tea to be ready. In front of her, Emanuel Lorreant sat in the big, brown lounge chair. He looked haggard and drained. His hair was messy, and he had grown out a considerable beard. Emanuel had been hiding in the basement of the boating club all along. An official police search had detected him munching on some hard piece of bread. Crouching in a corner, one of the officers first mistook him for a homeless transient who had broken into the place. Now he sat here, uncomfortable and eyeing everyone around him suspiciously. Anna and

Marcus Hepburn sat opposite him on the couch. They were holding each other's hands, unsure of what was going on. In the back to their left, leaning against the bookshelves was Adonis Markas. His arms crossed, he appeared on the verge of tears. Opposite him, on the divan by the door to the basement, gathered the Yavuz family. Hakan had his arm around Aylin while Murat stood behind them. He was squinting menacingly at everyone.

The atmosphere was as tense as it could be when Lagos and Selim set foot in the house. The Detective Inspector had ordered everyone to come here for a reason, one he was about to reveal. He knew that this was beyond unorthodox for standard police procedures. Then again, this case was anything but ordinary. Alas, by convening the suspects here, Lagos aimed to force long-buried emotions into the open, leveraging the intimate atmosphere to destabilize carefully constructed alibis. Moreover, the Detective Inspector firmly believed that in a setting so steeped in personal history, the tension between rivals and old grudges would compel the guilty to slip up. His carefully planned psychological trap where each suspect's past and present would collide unavoidably.

"What's the meaning of all of this?" asked Murat. Frustration dominated his tone. Lagos stepped forward, slightly moving into the center of it all.

"Thank you all very much for coming here on such short notice. Apologies to you, Mr. and Mrs. Lorreant, for choosing your house as the place of this gathering without elaborating on the reason too much. But I'm sure you'll understand soon enough.

Now, as young Mr. Yavuz has pointed out, why are we here? Let me provide you with an answer, to unmask a murderer."

"What's there to unmask? He's standing right next to us. Adonis is the man!" Marcus said and pointed at the man on his left.

"And why is that?" barked the accused. He seemed greatly offended by this charge.

"Oh, come on. We all know you never got over my wife. Your jealousy reeks up the entire room!"

"That's absurd!"

"Marcus is just trying to shift the blame! It was him, I'm sure of it. He killed my son out of pure hatred for my family," threw Hakan in angrily.

"What would I hate you for?" Mr. Hepburn returned, equally as heated.

"Everyone knows you sabotaged the construction plans of our house. You hate Turks, it's no secret!"

"For Christ's sake! Have you never moved on from this? You should seek help, you resentful moron," Marcus fumed.

Meanwhile, Emanuel Lorreant started laughing. It was a crazed, almost sad noise.

"What are you laughing at, pervert? We all know you're a crooked hillbilly! I bet my life savings that you're behind this," Anna shouted at him. Aylin cursed something in Turkish. Lagos assumed she was agreeing with her. Emanuel's laugh immediately stopped and turned into a snubbed grimace. In his condescending manner, he replied:

"You have no proof, you old hag."

"Don't I? Tell me, what makes you look more suspicious: that you're in charge of the local football team, or that you hire young boys to do the dirty work at the boating club."

Anna had spoken again.

"Cheap labor, that's all."

Before anyone could throw in any more wild and absurd accusations, Lagos tossed the Smith & Wesson Model 29 into the center of the living room. It landed with a loud thump.

"Are you giving up your job, or what's this move for?" scoffed Adonis. It was evident he was still blaming the Detective Inspector for his son's demise.

"Dirty Harry," Lagos said as if it was some grand answer to it all. Amélie was the first one to speak:

"Have you lost your mind?"

"Not at all, Mrs. Lorreant. In fact, I can see more clearly now than ever. Dirty Harry is a name of endearment for this type of revolver. It's the most commonly used gun on this island. The model you can see right here belongs to the murderer. But let's start at the beginning.

The accusations tossed around earlier, as outlandish as they might seem, aren't entirely baseless. For instance, while Adonis Markas is still secretly smitten with Anna Hepburn, he isn't responsible for Noah's death. Similarly, although Marcus Hepburn sabotaged the Yavuz family's housing project in his capacity as a city council member, that alone doesn't mark him as the murderer of young Kazim. And even though Mr. Lorreant's role as head of the local football club, and his dubious habit of hiring boys for menial tasks at the boating club, might cast a shadow of suspicion, it still isn't enough to nail him right away."

Lagos paused, letting the weight of his words settle in. "Our killer is an extraordinarily cunning individual, utterly devoid of empathy — a cold, calculating, and, in a perverse sense, lucky demon."

He then detailed the grim facts: "The first body we recovered was that of Kazim Yavuz. He was strangled, sexually assaulted, and then discarded into the sea. Later, civilians discovered him and left his body at the doorstep of the pristine hotel by the harbor." A tense murmur arose in the room. After a brief pause, Anna inquired, "Why does the order in which these acts were committed matter so much?"

Lagos leaned forward. "Because the sequence tells us how the killer operates. Strangulation came first, followed by assault, and finally disposal. Importantly, the assault occurred after death —

this detail isn't random; it speaks to the killer's ritualistic nature."

Murat pressed on, "And that ritual is what ultimately helps us narrow down our suspect?" Lagos's gaze swept across the room, the silence heavy with expectation as the truth began to unravel.

"Exactly! It tells us a lot about our killer. If the assault occurred before the murder, then the motive for kidnapping might be sexual in nature. An urge of some sort. Rape happening post-mortem is different. Why disgrace the person even more once they've already been killed? You see, a predator gets off on the thought of control, domination, and pain. For the aggressor to experience this, the victim must be alive, no? Considering that the sexual assaults happen after the killings gives us a different motive for the person we're looking for. Primarily, that these murders are not of a sexual nature. But rather, that it is an urge that follows after the deed has been done. I mean, think about it! Murdering a person must unleash an extraordinary amount of adrenaline in your body. There are, of course, different ways of combating such a surge. Some drink tea to calm down the nerves, others take up sports to clear their heads. Another option is to relieve oneself sexually. What I'm trying to get at; after the intense rush of killing someone, our killer ejaculates to release tension."

"That is beyond sickening!" Anna said and held a hand in front of her mouth. Marcus patted her back.

"You're right, Mrs. Hepburn. To us it is, to the killer, it is not. Either way, let us continue where I left off. After Kazim was discovered, our second victim turned up. Noah Hepburn. He, too, was first strangled, then raped, and finally thrown into the sea. At first, I thought these cases weren't connected at all until a friendly fisherman by the name of Nikos Zeniades confirmed that the boy had rope tied around his ankle during his discovery." At this point, Lagos threw in the white rope.

"Why is the rope so important?" Amélie asked.

"It's relevant for the timeline. As it turned out, Noah had been at the basin of the port the entire time. So, even though he had been missing considerably longer than Kazim, forensic reports showed that he was held the exact same amount of time as the first victim. In addition to that, both boys had been dressed up nicely after their deaths. It doesn't take an expert to see a pattern here. That was until a third boy, Paris Markas, turned up dead.

Even though the evidence pointed to all three cases being connected, it was only a well-founded suspicion until the death of this last victim tied things together. As it would turn out, Paris was missing an upper central incisor tooth. His original was surgically replaced with a fake. The same goes for Noah and Kazim."

"So what? Maybe they found themselves in some fight?" Emanuel injected.

"Did you not listen to what I just said? It was the exact same tooth for every child. A fist fight, one as you suggest, would result in different teeth being knocked out in each victim. No, the fact that all three missed an identical central incisor meant that our killer was collecting trophies. Something that could be conveniently achieved if one owned a surgical knife. In fact, the very knife you see right in front of you—" Lagos continued and threw in the knife. "Oh, and before I forget, these are the fake teeth we are talking about." He put them down. He had kept them in a small container, safely stored away in a bag. Everyone present gasped.

"At this point, we had established our suspect's profile, and we had understood the meaning of all items in front of you. All we needed to do now was to find the evidence that could identify our killer definitively."

"What more do you need? You have a gun, some rope, and a knife. Wherever these were found, determines who the killer is."

It was Murat who had intervened. He talked as if it was the most obvious thing in the world.

"Certainly, young Mr. Yavuz. But what if multiple people live in said house? Finding these things did help us narrow down our list of suspects from seven to two. These two being the very hosts of this gathering right now."

And with that, Lagos faced Mr. and Mrs. Lorreant. The entire delegation now turned on them. Emanuel had a big smile on his face, his eyes aimlessly circling around the ceiling. It was unclear if he hadn't paid any attention or was simply out of it. Perhaps, it had all been too much for him. Amélie, on the other hand, appeared shocked. With a hysteric scream, she quickly concluded:

"So it was my husband. He's the killer!"

"You ratty bitch!"

Selim chuckled. Murat, having smirked too at such a foul remark, got smacked by his mother for indecency. Anna and Adonis hadn't recovered from the turn of events just yet. Marcus was sitting silently with his arms and legs crossed.

"Now, now. No need for insults, Mr. Lorreant. After all, you did have multiple opportunities to snatch each and every one of those boys. Given also that you had a romantic relationship with our Adonis Markas does make you the ideal suspect. To further increase suspicion, you went into hiding as soon as things started to get heated. Combining all of these things together makes you, Emanuel, the perfect scapegoat.

Isn't it so, Amélie Lorreant?"

Lagos's eyes had now fixed on the woman still standing behind the kitchen counter. Emanuel made a face of deep complacency and turned around to face his wife.

"That's right! Emanuel Lorreant was purposely framed by his own wife for the murder of every victim. I mean, it was perfect, wasn't it? The only issue was that Emanuel Lorreant didn't have the right motives. As I said, the sexual assaults happened *after* the boys were killed. So if Mr. Lorreant wasn't, in fact, murdering the boys out of sexual desire, then what for? He didn't have any issues with the Yavuz, he was on good terms with the Hepburns, and he loved Adonis. What reason would he have?

The entire thing unveiled in front of me once the forensics office discovered that the victims were each missing a tooth. Mrs. Lorreant, do you remember how you told us about your childhood trauma? How you were made fun of as a child for having messed up teeth? Back then you could've just said, 'I knocked out my front teeth' but instead you opted for 'I knocked out my upper central incisor tooth' which is a medical term. The only people knowing this are dentists and people who have frequent issues with their dentures.

Overhearing your argument with a mother in your office only put the nail in the coffin. That lady, whose name wishes to be kept out of this, confronted you about making inappropriate advances toward her son during one of your therapy sessions. Once I had heard this, my fellow colleague Selim and I went into a deep dive into your life. And what we found was disturbing, to say the least.

For one, in your police file down by the station, there are multiple sexual misconduct felonies toward young boys. For reasons unclear to me, all of them were dropped eventually. The glory of corruption, I suppose. But they still remain sexual. Naturally, we immediately ordered a search warrant for your office and your house. Thanks to that, I was able to retrieve the gun, the rope, and the surgical knife. But that's not so much of importance now. What is relevant, however, is what Selim and I found in one of your desk drawers—neatly hidden beneath therapy files. Do you recognize this?"

With that, Lagos produced a dark, leathered book. It was worn and appeared to be frequently used. Amélie's eyes widened, and all color left her face.

"It's a diary for those who don't know. In it, Mrs. Lorreant goes into excruciating detail about each boy she fancied. In particular, Noah Hepburn. The notes go on to describe how beautiful he is and that you have touched yourself to the thought of him repeatedly. However, there is one specific paragraph I'd like to read to you today."

"That's not necessary!"

"Please don't."

Ignoring all appeals, Lagos cleared his throat and began with:

"'I killed Noah today. I couldn't contain my urges anymore, so I took him and played with him. It was breathtaking. I had to get rid of him. The depths of the ocean will keep my secret'. Reading this, it was urgent to find out if you had an alibi for the day Noah went missing. I talked to Mrs. Hepburn to see if you were present at Pilates when Noah was kidnapped. She denied it, saying that you had called in sick. Mrs. Hepburn also mentioned that this behavior was odd, as you never missed a single class.

Mrs. Lorreant knew Noah would be there. After all, Mrs. Hepburn brought him along every time. So, supposedly sick, she still turned up to the lesson and led Noah away to her car. The janitor observed it. He told Selim and me after the little gathering we had there recently, remember? There's no denying it."

"So the motive was sexual of nature?" Hakan interjected.

"I'll get to the motive shortly, Mr. Yavuz. Now, during the disposal of Noah Hepburn, which was cleverly done, fate would have it that Kazim Yavuz observed her. Murat and Kazim had been raiding the basement of the boating club for fishing gear that night. Understanding that she had been caught, Mrs. Lorreant quickly reacted by following the boys home. On their way, Kazim noticed that they were being followed and pointed it out to his older brother, Murat. Who, in turn, dismissed it as a fear of the dark. A fatal mistake.

Once at the house, Amélie Lorreant knocked on Kazim's window. The poor boy, unaware of the imminent danger he was in, opened up as he recognized her face. After all, he knew her as this friendly woman from the boating club. No way in hell would she harm him. Most likely, Kazim expected their stalker to be a man, and so was not on his guard when Mrs. Lorreant asked him to follow her. She probably told him that she had observed them stealing from the club, and if she just got her share, then she wouldn't tell his parents. So Kazim obliged. Soon after, the boy was found by the harbor.

Then, something peculiar happened. For weeks, no other boy turned up dead until, suddenly, Paris Markas was found murdered. It bears the question of why? Why kill another boy if the entire island is on high alert, and so far, you have gotten away with it?

The answer is simple. Mrs. Lorreant had caught wind of her husband's adultery. A letter from Adonis breaking things off with Emanuel showed her that he had been sharing the bed with someone else. In a fit of rage, she kidnapped Paris during one of her therapy sessions. After all, the boy was seeing her regularly for his stutter treatment. And there you have it; three different motives for three different murders."

"So what exactly are the motives? I'm confused," Adonis interjected.

He had been crying.

"The first victim, Noah Hepburn, was sexually motivated. The second one, Kazim Yavuz, was collateral damage — excuse my harsh expression —, and the third one, Paris Markas, was an act of revenge on her husband and his lover.

Raping her victims is just a part of Mrs. Lorreant's demons. As I said earlier, it is a reaction to a large amount of bodily pressure. Most likely, Mrs. Lorreant even felt guilty for what she did afterward. It is the reason she put such good care into her victims' appearance post-mortem. All three murders had a motherly touch to them. As disturbing as this sounds, it is something that stood out to me from the very first minute." With that, Lagos concluded his monologue. After a moment of deliberation, Murat brought forward:

"But what about the footprint found by our house?"

"Oh, that? I forgot to mention it! The footprint belonged to Mr. Hepburn. Grudges never truly fade, I reckon. He was prying around the house earlier that day, hoping for a way to expose his rival. If the Yavuz family was forced to move away, he could buy their house for cheap and turn it into a hotel. That was his initial plan for the piece of land, which has nothing to do with the murders, however," Lagos explained.

Marcus nodded approvingly, shifting everyone's focus on Amélie Lorreant. Shrugging her shoulders, she explained:

"Jig's up, I guess. I could neither physically punish my husband nor Adonis for what they did. So I took away and tainted what both adored most."

Emanuel started to cry.

"See, Detective Inspector, I fell in love with Noah the first time I saw him during Pilates. Especially his beautiful smile. At first, I didn't know how to feel about this. I knew it was wrong, but my urges kept coming back. I knew I needed to satisfy them; otherwise, I'd lose my mind. I treated him well, too. I kept him chained to a heater in the basement with plenty of food and water. I even provided a blanket and a cushion. He had everything he needed, but then I caught him trying to run away, so I had to do what needed to be done. Seeing the life fade out of his beautiful eyes broke my heart. I cried until I ran dry of tears.

Kazim, as you said, caught me in the act of disposal. The boy looked terrified, and I knew he probably wouldn't tell a single soul about this. But I couldn't run the risk. Kazim was incredibly vigilant. He even noticed me tailing them. It was thanks to his naive brother that it all went through smoothly. When he saw my face at the window, he beamed. It was the easiest thing in the world to talk him into following me. I simply had to offer up a tiny wooden boat in exchange —"The one we had found in his room!", Aylin threw in. — I got it when I was a child myself. Once we were in my car, heading out of Adamantas, I think he started to realize that I was the one who had been following him. Especially when he saw the Dirty Harry on the passenger-side dashboard. You should've seen the terror in his eyes.

You described me as a heartless demon earlier, Detective Inspector. I take great offense to that. I was blatantly aware of taking an innocent child's life simply because he had been in the wrong place at the wrong time. I didn't enjoy any of that, not that this justifies anything. Nonetheless, I swore I wouldn't kill another soul and banished my demons.

But then my idiotic husband had to cheat on me. You couldn't imagine the shame and hatred I felt. The day after I had found the letter, that arrogant little Paris sat across from me stuttering in therapy. It completely unhinged my demons. It was as if they had taken control of my mind and body. I can't even remember how I subdued and took him from my office. I can't even recall dropping him into the ocean.

I knew right away that you were trailing me. Once I had found out about my husband's affair, I conceived the plan to put a false trail on him. This way, I could punish him even further for what he did to me while covering up my own tracks. It would've worked out so well if it wasn't for you, Detective Inspector Lagos."

The man looked far from being complimented. Dionisis appeared sad and thoughtful.

"You took the children's teeth out of jealousy, didn't you?", he asked, knowing the answer already.

"Yes. It's true, ever since I got bullied in school I've had this insane insecurity about my teeth. Noah, Kazim, and Paris had all such perfect smiles, never the need for braces. Even in death, they laughed at me with their flawless little mouths. I had to do something about it. From all of my own visits to the dentist, I knew damn well how to remove a tooth. Especially from a body that can't defend itself anymore."

"Then why did you place a prosthesis in each of them afterward? Why did you drop them in the water by the harbor? Why that location?"

"For the same reason, I dressed them up nicely. I felt guilty for what I did. I hoped the beautiful water would rinse their bodies clean. And perhaps my sins along with them."

With his gaze on the gun, rope, and surgical knife, the Detective Inspector threw his handcuffs onto the pile.

.

EPILOGUE

Small, consistent drops fell from the ceiling when Amélie Lorreant was thrown into her prison cell. She grazed the palms of her hands when she stumbled to the ground. In the gloom of the room, a giggle echoed.

"Who's there?" Amélie asked, frightened.

"Tell me, has the high and mighty Detective Inspector put you here?"

"Dionisis Lagos? Yes, why?"

Out of the darkness stepped Helena Kostea. With a crazed, menacing stare, she declared:

"Because it is time for us to take our revenge!"

The turquoise-green waves rippled against the wooden boat. Somewhere in the distance, seagulls could be heard squawking. The smell of caramelizing meat mingled with the smoke of drifts and salty air. The sky was in hues of orange, yellow, and gold. Men and women alike could be heard chatting and laughing. A live band was playing Greek-Turkish-influenced tunes. Dionisis Lagos was munching on a loukoumade, a type of deep-fried donut. He was drunk. His roaring laugh carried across the seven seas as a party guest sat to his right, telling a funny story. On his left was Selim, chatting with Dr. Eleni Castella. She was evidently trying to get a more exclusive experience. It didn't change the fact that she vehemently disapproved of all the people roaming the boat. She wasn't exactly the party-goer, but Lagos had insisted on celebrating their arrest of Amélie Lorreant.

After Mrs. Lorreant had confessed to the killings, police forces, having been notified, stormed the house and arrested her. It was a devastating scene to witness. She hadn't put up a fight at all. In fact, she picked up Lagos' handcuffs from the ground and put them on her own wrists. On her way out, her eyes lingered on Selim. The latter held eye contact. Lagos supposed he was showing his confidence in their justice system. Either way, when Amélie walked past the Detective Inspector, who stood by the door at this point, she gave him a spiteful glance. Meanwhile, Aylin Yavuz had started to cry, and Murat needed to be contained by Hakan from assaulting Amélie Lorreant. In a rush, the young man had picked up the Dirty Harry to point it at his brother's killer.

The Hepburns immediately fled the scene, retreating to their house. Marcus was worried about the entire incident affecting his reputation as a city councilman. After all, re-elections were due in the fall. Anna, who hadn't been aware of Adonis' feelings at all, wanted to save herself the awkwardness of confronting him about it and instead dodged it gladly. Adonis Markas, on the other hand, unsure of whether to follow Anna or try talking to Emanuel, simply buried his face in his hands. Minutes later, Emanuel came and touched his shoulder lovingly. This action didn't have the intended effect at all, as it prompted Adonis to punch the man in the face. Revolted by Emanuel, he apparently wasn't feeling as strongly for the fellow anymore as he once did. Immediately, two police officers slammed Adonis Markas against the bookshelves and handcuffed him. He was dragged out and put on the seat next to Amélie soon after. Emanuel Lorreant, hurt and confused, fled for the basement once more.

'They quarrel and mingle like a bunch of children. Even their dead sons would've handled this situation better, Lagos thought as he observed it all.

Now, talking about it to other people made the incident look like a scene from a comic book. Selim agreed when Lagos shared his thoughts. Dr. Eleni Castella had excused herself for the bathroom, winking at Selim on her way over there. It was evidently an invitation to follow her.

"What are you waiting for?"

"Something is holding me back, Abi. I just don't know what it is."

"Just go after her! What do the worries of the world matter, as long as you have good food and even better company?" Lagos laughed before roaring:

"After all, there are only two things every man must truly love; wine and women!"

A special thank you to Debbi, as well as my friends and family

DOLOR

1946, New York

Tom, a charming and ambitious young man, embarks on a promising career at the New York Police Department. Alongside his thriving personal life, he encounters the enchanting Emily at his closest friend's wedding, leading them to fall deeply in love.

Yet, as Tom's career flourishes, he becomes entangled in a series of perplexing and seemingly unsolvable murders. Additionally, the rise in influence of a menacing gang poses a significant threat, potentially shattering Tom's glamorous path. The supposed loss of his beloved Emily could push him to the brink of his mental stability, a place engulfed by nothing but shadows and despair.

CURRENTLY ONLY AVAILABLE IN GERMAN

DILITIRIO

Milos: an island where the light blue Aegean waters clash against golden beaches. A place whose natural beauty hides dark tales. Some of which are better left untold. When the lifeless naked body of a Swiss tourist is discovered, hedonistic Inspector Dionisis Lagos is assigned to the case. But the task of solving this eerie tragedy proves to be far from easy, as it threatens to throw the island into destructive chaos...

Unbeknownst to most but crucial to this tale lies a forgotten artifact known as the apple of Hephaestus.

TIMUR E. SIMSEK

Timur E. Simsek lives in Bern, Switzerland. He spent most of his childhood immersed in fiction and crafting short stories. At twenty-three, he released his debut novel, *Dolor*, which was soon followed by his second work, *Dilitirio*. His passions extend beyond writing to include history, Greek mythology, and cultural studies. He is currently pursuing a master's degree in English Literature at the University of Zurich.

Katara marks his third book.